E.T.A. HOFFMANN'S

The Nutcracker and the Mouse King

THE GRAPHIC NOVEL

Illustrated & Adapted by

NATALIE ANDREWSON

First Second
New York

Table of Contents

ONCE UPON A TIME...
...THERE WAS A BEAUTIFUL PRINCESS...
...WHO LOVED TO LET HER IMAGINATION WANDER.
CREEEAAAKKKK!
BUT SHE WAS PLAGUED...

...BY NIGHTMARES!
CRACK!
CRACK!
CREAK!
GASP!
AHHH!
TRIP!
OOOF!
AAAHHH!!!

AHHHHHHH!!
...
Oh.
Chapter One
CHRISTMAS EVE
ALL DAY ON DECEMBER THE TWENTY-FOURTH, THE CHILDREN OF DOCTOR STAHLBAUM WERE NOT PERMITTED TO ENTER THE DINING ROOM, MUCH LESS THE ADJOINING LIVING ROOM.

FRITZ AND MARIE WERE CONFINED IN THE BACK ROOM WITH NO CANDLES.
THIS WAS CUSTOMARY IN GERMANY ON CHRISTMAS EVE...
...EVEN AS NIGHT WAS SETTING IN AND THEIR SHADOWS BEGAN TO GROW.
THEY HAD BEEN WAITING VERY PATIENTLY ALL DAY...
HMM...
CREAAK
OOMF
...AND WERE SUDDENLY FEELING MUCH MORE ANXIOUS IN THE CREEPING DARKNESS.

PSST, MARIE...
I HAVE A SECRET TO TELL YOU.
I'VE BEEN HEARING STRANGE RUSTLING NOISES COMING FROM DOWNSTAIRS ALL DAY...
Ka-ling!
...AND JUST NOW I SAW THE SHADOW OF A SMALL MAN SLIPPING A BOX UNDER HIS ARM!
Ka-ling!
IT HAS TO BE GODFATHER DROSSELMEIER!
REALLY?! OH, I WONDER WHAT SPECIAL PRESENTS GODFATHER DROSSELMEIER HAS MADE FOR US THIS YEAR!

NOW, THE CHIEF JUSTICE DROSSELMEIER WAS NOT A VERY PRETTY MAN.
WHERE HIS RIGHT EYE OUGHT TO HAVE BEEN HE WORE A LARGE BLACK EYEPATCH. HE HAD NO HAIR ON HIS HEAD, SO HE WORE A BEAUTIFULLY HANDCRAFTED WHITE WIG THAT LOOKED LIKE IT WAS MADE OF GLASS.
HE WAS QUITE SMALL AND SKINNY AND HAD MANY WRINKLES ON HIS FACE AND HANDS.
BUT WHAT HE LACKED IN BEAUTY, HE MADE UP FOR IN CLEVERNESS.
HE WAS A MECHANICALLY MINDED MAN AND KNEW A GREAT DEAL ABOUT WATCHES AND CLOCKS...
...EVEN KNOWING HOW TO MAKE THEM HIMSELF.
WHEN ONE OF THE BEAUTIFUL CLOCKS IN DR. STAHLBAUM'S HOUSE STOPPED WORKING PROPERLY...
Hmm.
...GODFATHER DROSSELMEIER WOULD COME TO FIX IT.

HE'D TAKE OFF HIS WIG AND HIS COAT AND RETREAT TO THE STAHLBAUMS' ATTIC, WHICH THEY'D GIVEN TO HIM AS HIS PERSONAL WORKSHOP.
THERE HE'D WORK ON THE CLOCKS FOR HOURS WITH POINTED INSTRUMENTS UNTIL HE FOUND THE ROOT OF THE PROBLEM.
MARIE WAS VERY DISTRESSED BY ALL THE PAINS HE MUST HAVE BEEN CAUSING THE CLOCKS, BUT THE CLOCKS WEREN'T HURT AT ALL!
RATHER, THEY WOULD COME TO LIFE AGAIN AND PURR AND BEAT AS JOYFULLY AS EVER...
...MUCH TO MARIE'S RELIEF.

DROSSELMEIER ALWAYS BROUGHT SOMETHING NICE IN HIS COAT POCKETS FOR THE CHILDREN WHEN HE CAME TO VISIT.
ONCE HE BROUGHT A LITTLE MAN WHO ROLLED HIS EYES AND BOWED.
AND ONCE HE BROUGHT A BOX WITH A LITTLE BIRD INSIDE THAT WOULD HOP OUT.
HIS GIFTS WERE ALWAYS A DELIGHTFUL MYSTERY.
EVERY CHRISTMAS HE MADE SOMETHING SPECTACULAR FOR THE CHILDREN, ALWAYS COSTING HIM A GREAT DEAL OF TROUBLE AND EFFORT.
THOSE GIFTS WERE USUALLY PUT ASIDE FOR SAFEKEEPING BY THE STAHLBAUM CHILDREN'S PARENTS.
WHAT DO YOU THINK IT COULD BE THIS TIME?

MAYBE HE'LL BRING A GREAT FORTRESS WITH UNIFORMED SOLDIERS WHO GUARD THE KEEPS!
IT'LL DEPICT A GREAT WAR!
AND ALL THE BRAVE SOLDIERS WILL SHOOT THEIR CANNONS TO KEEP INTRUDERS AWAY!
BANG!
BOOM!
NO, NO! GODFATHER DROSSELMEIER PROMISED ME A BEAUTIFUL GARDEN!
IT HAS A GREAT LAKE WHERE BEAUTIFUL SWANS SING THE PRETTIEST SONGS.
THE MAIDEN WHO LIVES THERE LIKES TO LURE THE SWANS WITH SWEET MARZIPAN!
SWANS DON'T EAT MARZIPAN!
GODFATHER CAN'T MAKE YOU A WHOLE GARDEN. A FORTRESS IS MUCH MORE REALISTIC.
IT DOESN'T MATTER ANYWAY, THEY ALWAYS TAKE AWAY THE GIFTS HE BRINGS US.
I'D RATHER GET TOYS FROM MAMA AND PAPA. WE CAN KEEP THOSE AND DO WHAT WE WANT WITH THEM.
HMM...
PAPA KNOWS VERY WELL THAT I'M MISSING IMPORTANT SCOUTS AND HUSSARS IN MY ARMY.
I DO LOVE TO PLAY WITH THE GIFTS MAMA GIVES ME.

I'D ALSO LIKE A FOX AND A DRUMMER.
OOPS.
POP!
SHH! DO YOU HEAR THAT?!
THERE'S MUSIC COMING FROM THE PARLOR! IT'S SO PRETTY!
SWOOSH
COME, COME, DEAR CHILDREN!
COME AND SEE WHAT FATHER CHRISTMAS HAS BROUGHT YOU THIS YEAR!
Ooooh!! Ahhh!

Chapter Two
THE GIFTS
THE CHILDREN MUST HAVE BEEN VERY GENEROUS AND GOOD ALL YEAR 'ROUND...
...BECAUSE THEY HAD NEVER BEFORE RECEIVED SO MANY BEAUTIFUL GIFTS ON CHRISTMAS EVE.

OH! LOOK AT THESE!
OH, HOW BEAUTIFUL!
MAY I PUT IT ON? MAY I REALLY WEAR IT?!
THIS IS SUCH A WILD HORSE! I'LL HAVE TO TRAIN HIM!
OOHH!
AAHH!
Ka-ling Ka-ling

IN ALL THE COMMOTION AND DELIGHT OF CHRISTMAS EVE...
Ka-ling
Ka-ling
AHEM!
...THE CHILDREN HAD NOT EVEN SEEN DROSSELMEIER IN THE CORNER.
TUG!
HE SUDDENLY PULLED A LONG STRING FROM A CURTAIN HE HAD HUNG FROM THE CEILING...
OH!!!
...AND FINALLY REVEALED THE MOST ANTICIPATED GIFT OF THE NIGHT: HIS MYSTERY PRESENT FOR THE CHILDREN.

DROSSELMEIER HAD CREATED A CONTRAPTION THAT DELIGHTED BOTH THE CHILDREN, FOR HE HAD TAKEN INTO CONSIDERATION BOTH OF THEIR CHRISTMAS WISHES.
THERE WERE FRITZ'S SOLDIERS, PREPARING FOR BATTLE AND GUARDING THE FORTRESS. AND THERE WAS MARIE'S BEAUTIFUL PALACE GARDEN, COMPLETE WITH SWANS, JUST AS SHE'D REQUESTED.
THEY WATCHED IN AWE AS THE LITTLE CHARACTERS MOVED IN AND OUT OF THE CASTLE.
FRITZ WAS ENTHRALLED. HE LOVED WATCHING THE SOLDIERS MOVE ABOUT THE TOWERS, EVEN THOUGH HE WISHED THERE WAS A MOAT INSTEAD OF A SILLY SWAN GARDEN.

BUT THEN FRITZ BEGAN TO REALIZE...
...THE SOLDIERS WERE JUST DOING THE SAME THING, OVER AND OVER AGAIN.
HE QUICKLY BECAME BORED.
GODFATHER, CAN YOU OPEN THE CASTLE SO I CAN SEE INSIDE?
I'M AFRAID THAT IS QUITE IMPOSSIBLE, YOUNG FRITZ.
WELL, THEN CAN YOU MAKE THE SOLDIERS WALK THROUGH THE GARDENS THIS TIME?
I CANNOT DO THAT, NO.
THEN...CAN YOU AT LEAST MAKE THEM SHOOT THEIR CANNONS?
THAT CANNOT BE DONE, FRITZ.

BUT I WANT THEM TO DO SOMETHING MORE! SOLDIERS DON'T JUST WALK AROUND! I WANT TO PLAY WITH THEM!
FRITZ! IT'S SIMPLY IMPOSSIBLE! THE MECHANICS WERE MADE THIS WAY AND SO THIS WAY THEY MUST REMAIN!
LISTEN, GODFATHER DROSSELMEIER, IF YOUR LITTLE FIGURES CAN ONLY DO THE SAME THING OVER AND OVER AGAIN...
...THEN THEY'RE USELESS TO ME!
Argh.
I'D RATHER PLAY WITH MY HUSSARS HERE. I CAN MOVE THEM BACK AND FORTH AS I PLEASE, JUST LIKE REAL SOLDIERS. THEY'RE NOT SOME BORING MACHINE!

AN INGENIOUS WORK LIKE THIS WAS NOT MADE FOR CHILDREN!
I'M PACKING THIS UP AND CARRYING IT HOME RIGHT NOW!
OH, DO STAY, COUNSELOR. WE'D LOVE TO SEE HOW IT WORKS.
Hmm...
Humph!
WELL...
...I SUPPOSE I COULD SHARE SOME OF MY SECRETS.
Ka-ling ka-ling
WHAT'S THIS?

Chapter Three
THE FAVORITE
MARIE STOPPED IN FRONT OF THE CHRISTMAS TREE, TRANSFIXED, FOR SHE HAD DISCOVERED A GIFT UPON WHICH NO ONE HAD YET REMARKED.
FRITZ HAD MOVED ALL HIS HUSSARS AND SOLDIERS FROM BENEATH THE TREE, REVEALING A CURIOUS LITTLE MAN. HE STOOD THERE SILENT, AS IF HE WERE WAITING PATIENTLY FOR HIS TURN TO BE NOTICED.

IT MUST BE CONFESSED, NOT MUCH COULD BE SAID IN FAVOR OF THE BEAUTY OF HIS FIGURE.
NOT ONLY WAS HIS STOUT BODY OUT OF PROPORTION TO HIS SLIM LITTLE LEGS, BUT HIS HEAD WAS FAR TOO LARGE FOR EITHER.
HIS GENTEEL COAT DID A GREAT DEAL TO COMPENSATE FOR THESE SHORTCOMINGS AND LED TO THE BELIEF THAT HE MUST BE A MAN OF GOOD TASTE.
IN ADDITION TO HIS HANDSOME APPAREL, HE HAD HUNG UPON HIS BACK A NARROW, CLUMSY CLOAK, AND UPON HIS HEAD HE WORE A WOODSMAN'S CAP.
MARIE COULD NOT HELP BUT THINK THAT EVEN IF GODFATHER DROSSELMEIER WERE AS WELL DRESSED AS THIS LITTLE MAN, HE WOULD STILL NOT LOOK HALF AS HANDSOME.

THE LONGER MARIE GAZED UPON THE TINY MAN, WHOM SHE CHERISHED AT FIRST SIGHT, THE MORE FRIENDLY AND GOOD-NATURED HIS FACE SEEMED TO LOOK.

THOUGH LARGE AND QUITE PROTRUDING, HIS CLEAR EYES SHONE WITH NOTHING BUT KINDNESS.

IT WAS A GOOD THING HE WORE A WELL-TRIMMED, COTTON-WHITE BEARD, LYING AROUND HIS CHIN LIKE SNOW, FOR HIS SWEET RED CHEEKS COULD BE APPRECIATED ALL THE MORE.

FATHER, WHO DOES THIS CHARMING LITTLE MAN BY THE TREE BELONG TO?
??
WELL, HE CAN BELONG TO BOTH YOU AND FRITZ EQUALLY.
MARIE, SINCE YOUR NEW FRIEND IS SO SPECIAL TO YOU, I HEREBY PLACE HIM UNDER YOUR PARTICULAR CARE.
HOWEVER, YOU MUST STILL SHARE HIM WITH FRITZ IF HE ASKS.
HERE, PLACE A NUT INSIDE HIS MOUTH AND SEE WHAT HAPPENS.
CRRACK!
HE'S A NUTCRACKER!
HE DESCENDS FROM A LONG LINE OF HARD WORKERS...
...AND PRACTICES THE PROFESSION OF HIS ANCESTORS.

WHAT A SILLY LITTLE MAN!
I WANT TO TRY!
GIVE ME THAT!
CCRAACK!
CREAK!
I WANT HIM TO CRACK ALL THE LARGEST WALNUTS FOR ME AND MY SOLDIERS!
CRRUNNCHH
HUH?
NO!
SNNAPP!

AH! MY POOR, DEAR NUTCRACKER!
SNATCH!
OBVIOUSLY HE ISN'T VERY GOOD AT HIS JOB.
HE WANTS TO BE A NUTCRACKER BUT DOESN'T UNDERSTAND HIS CRAFT AT ALL.
WHY ARE YOU MAKING SUCH A FUSS ABOUT HIM?
GIVE HIM TO ME, MARIE!
NO, NO! YOU CAN'T HAVE HIM!
JUST LOOK AT HIM! HE LOOKS SO SAD. YOU'VE BROKEN HIS JAW!
PFFFT!!
BUT YOU'RE A HARD-HEARTED PERSON. YOU ALWAYS BEAT YOUR HORSES, AND RECENTLY YOU SHOT ONE OF YOUR OWN SOLDIERS! I WOULDN'T EXPECT YOU TO UNDERSTAND!
YOU KNOW NOTHING ABOUT WAR!
AND IT DOESN'T MATTER BECAUSE THE NUTCRACKER BELONGS TO BOTH ME AND YOU, SO GIVE HIM HERE!
WAAAAAH!

IT'S JUST A NUTCRACKER...
I THINK FRITZ SHOULD BE ABLE TO PLAY WITH IT HOW HE PLEASES.
THERE, THERE.
SNIFF
SNIFF
THANK YOU, GODFATHER.
NOW, I HAVE PLACED THE NUTCRACKER EXPRESSLY UNDER MARIE'S PROTECTION, AND, AS I SEE IT, HE NEEDS HER NOW.
SNIFFF
I THEREFORE GRANT MARIE FULL POWER AND AUTHORITY OVER HIM, SO NO ONE MAY DISPUTE IT.
I AM VERY SURPRISED BY YOU, FRITZ.
IT'S OBVIOUS THAT THIS SOLDIER REQUIRES MEDICAL ATTENTION.
HUH.
A GOOD GENERAL SHOULD KNOW THAT WOUNDED SOLDIERS ARE NEVER EXPECTED ON THE BATTLEFIELD, AND LEAST OF ALL ON THE FRONT LINES.

MARIE, HOW COULD YOU CHERISH SUCH AN UGLY FELLOW? HA-HA!
WHO KNOWS, DEAR GODFATHER— IF YOU DRESSED AS NICELY AS MY SWEET NUTCRACKER AND WERE AS WELL-KEPT AS HIM...
...WOULD YOU LOOK EVEN HALF AS PRETTY?
SNICKER
ooh!
SNICKER
MARIE COULD NOT TELL WHY HER PARENTS LAUGHED SO LOUDLY AT THIS, THOUGH THERE MUST HAVE BEEN SOME REASON FOR IT.

Chapter Four
WONDERS UPON WONDERS
JUST AS ONE ENTERED THE STAHLBAUM HOUSE, THERE STOOD ON THE LEFT-HAND SIDE A HIGH GLASS CASE IN WHICH THE CHILDREN KEPT ALL THE BEAUTIFUL TOYS GIVEN TO THEM EACH YEAR.
ON THE UPPER SHELF, WHICH MARIE AND FRITZ WERE UNABLE TO REACH, SAT ALL THE CHILDREN'S BEAUTIFUL PICTURE BOOKS.
IMMEDIATELY BELOW THIS WAS THE SHELF FOR GODFATHER DROSSELMEIER'S CURIOUS MACHINES...

...AND THE TWO SHELVES ON THE BOTTOM WERE RESERVED FOR MARIE AND FRITZ TO FILL AS THEY PLEASED.
IT ALWAYS HAPPENED THAT MARIE USED THE LOWER ONE TO HOUSE HER DOLLS, WHILE FRITZ STATIONED HIS TROOPS IN THE ONE ABOVE.
AFTER THE EXCITEMENT OF CHRISTMAS EVE HAD COME TO A CLOSE, MARIE WENT TO HER RESPECTIVE SHELF AND BEGAN TO SET UP ALL HER PRESENTS.
MARIE'S NEW DOLL, MISS CLARETTE, LOOKED RIGHT AT HOME IN MARIE'S NICELY FURNISHED SHELF.

IT WAS NOW VERY LATE IN THE EVENING. DROSSELMEIER HAD GONE HOME A LONG TIME BEFORE. AND YET THE CHILDREN WERE STILL AWAKE.
TIME FOR BED, CHILDREN.
YOU'RE RIGHT, THESE POOR HUSSARS NEED TO SLEEP. AND THEY WOULDN'T DARE NOD OFF WHILE I'M HERE.
GOOD NIGHT, MEN.
OH, PLEASE LET ME STAY A LITTLE WHILE LONGER, MOTHER.
I HAVE JUST A FEW THINGS LEFT, AND WHEN I'M DONE I'LL GO TO BED AT ONCE!
MARIE WAS A TRUSTWORTHY CHILD, SO HER MOTHER LET HER STAY IN THE FOYER. BUT FOR FEAR SHE MIGHT FORGET THE CANDLES, WHICH BURNED AROUND HER, MOTHER BLEW THEM ALL OUT.
FWOOOOOOOOOOO
SHE LEFT ONLY THE CANDLES THAT HUNG FROM THE CEILING AND DIFFUSED A SOFT, PLEASANT LIGHT.
COME TO BED SOON, MY DEAR, SO YOU CAN WAKE UP EARLY TOMORROW MORNING.
YES, MAMA.

MARIE HAD IN MIND ONE TASK SHE STILL NEEDED TO COMPLETE.
SHE PULLED OUT THE WOUNDED NUTCRACKER, WRAPPED IN HER RIBBON, AND LAID HIM CAREFULLY UPON THE TABLE TO EXAMINE HIS WOUNDS.
OH, NUTCRACKER, DON'T BE ANGRY WITH FRITZ. HE DIDN'T MEAN TO BE SO ROUGH, I'M SURE OF IT.
IT'S HIS WILD SOLDIER'S LIFE WITH HIS HUSSARS THAT MAKES HIM SO RUDE.
OTHERWISE, HE'S A GOOD BROTHER, I CAN ASSURE YOU. NOW, I'LL TEND TO THIS WOUND SO YOU CAN BE HAPPY AGAIN.
GODFATHER DROSSELMEIER WILL FIX YOU UP PROPERLY SOON, OF COURSE. HE KNOWS HOW TO FIX ANYTHING.
GASP!
YOUR EYES!

MAYBE IT WAS JUST THE LIGHT FLICKERING...
I'M NOT SCARED SO EASILY.
WOODEN DOLLS DON'T MAKE FACES!
NOW, MISS CLARETTE, WOULD YOU BE SO KIND AS TO GIVE UP YOUR BED FOR OUR INJURED FRIEND NUTCRACKER, AND MOVE TO THE SOFA FOR THE TIME BEING?
REMEMBER THAT YOU ARE VERY HEALTHY OR ELSE YOU WOULDN'T HAVE SUCH ROSY CHEEKS!
BESIDES, VERY FEW DOLLS HAVE SUCH NICE SOFAS AS YOURS.
SO SELFISH, MISS CLARETTE! IF YOU WON'T MOVE, THEN I'LL HAVE TO MOVE YOU MYSELF!
HMMM... WHAT ELSE CAN I DO...

AH, YES. YOU CAN'T STAY WITH NAUGHTY CLARETTE WHO'S UPSET AND WANTS HER BED BACK!
YOU'LL BE RIGHT AT HOME WITH FRITZ'S ARMY.
DONE.
LOCK
PITTER PATTER PITTER
PITTER
YAWN
PATTER PITTER PATTER PITTER PATTER
PATTER
PITTER
PATTER
PITTER

RUMBLE! RUMBLE!
RUMBLE
RUMBLE RUMBLE!
WWHIRRR
WWWHIRR
WWWHIRRRRRRRR
WHIRRR
WWHIRRRR
WHIRRR
WHIRRRRRR
VWOOOOOOOOM!
BEAT!
FLAP!
WWWHIRRRRRRRR

WHICH WATCH, CLICK AND CLOCK...
THE MICE, THE MICE ARE STIRRING...
TIME, CHIME, TICK AND TOCK...
HE WAKES, HE LIKES THE PURRING!
WHIRR
WOO GOOOOOOOOOOOOOOOOO
WOOOOOOOOOO HNG
IT SINGS FOR HIM, IT CALLS MOUSE KING!
PURR-UMM PURR-UM PURRUMM!
HE DRAWS EVER NEARER EACH TIME IT RINGS!
BURR-UMM BURR-UMUMM!
STRIKE!!
STRIKE!!
AND SOON FOR HIM THIS SONG WILL STING!
AAHHHHHHH!!!

Ka-ling
Ka-ling
GONG!
GONG!
GONG!
GONG!
GONG
GONG
GONG
GONG
GONG
GONG
GONG
GONG!!

GODFATHER DROSSELMEIER?!
WHAT ARE YOU DOING UP THERE?!
GET DOWN FROM THERE RIGHT NOW!
YOU CAN'T FRIGHTEN ME, NAUGHTY GODFATHER!
AWAKE, AWAKE!
AWAKE! AWAKE! HE KNOWS THE TIME!
AWAKE, AWAKE AT THE TWELFTH CHIME!

SSSSSQUEAK!!!!
SQUEAK!
SQUEAK!
SQUEAK!
SQUEAK!
SQUEAK!
SQUEAK!
SQUEAK
SQUEAK
SQUEAK
SQUEAK!
SQUEAK!
SQUEAK!
HMM?
NOW WHAT IS THIS, DROSSELMEIER?
I'M NOT AFRAID OF LITTLE MI—
—CE?
SQUEAK!

RUMBLE
RUMBLE
RUMBLE
RUMBLE
RUMBLE
RUMBLE
SSSCREEEAAACH!!
THUD
HUH?

AHH!
STUMBLE
STUMBLE
CRASH!
AT THAT MOMENT MARIE FELT A SHARP PAIN IN HER LEFT ARM, AND YET HER HEART FELT MUCH LIGHTER.
SHE HEARD NO MORE SQUEAKING AND SQUEALING. EVERYTHING HAD BECOME STILL.
IT WAS OVER.
THE FOYER SEEMED TO RETURN TO NORMAL AS THE CLOCK STRUCK MIDNIGHT.
BONG
BONG
BONG
BONG

AND YET...
AWAKE, FRIENDS AND BROTHERS! AWAKE, AWAKE BY CANDLELIGHT!
UP, UP, AWAKE, AWAKE! TO THE FIGHT, TO THE FIGHT! AWAKE, AWAKE!
WE WILL DRIVE BACK THOSE AWFUL MICE! NOW STAND WITH ME ON THIS EPIC NIGHT!
YES, YES, COMMANDER NUTCRACKER! WE'D MARCH FOR YOU AGAINST ANY FOE! MOUSE KING AND HIS ARMY WILL NOT BREAK OUR ROWS!
THEN TO BATTLE WE GO!
NO!
NUTCRACKER! YOU'RE TOO HURT!

OH NO! NUTCRACKER, BE CAREFUL!
LEAP
OOF!
I'LL SAVE YOU, NUTCRACKER!
GASP!
OH! MISS CLARETTE! HOW I'VE UNDERESTIMATED YOU! YOU'RE SUCH A GOOD DOLL!
OOMF
DO NOT GO INTO BATTLE, SWEET NUTCRACKER!
I MUST GO!
NNOOOOOOO!
MY LADY, PLEASE!
TAKE MY HANDKERCHIEF TO REMEMBER ME BY, SWEET NUTCRACKER!
ALAS, I MUST DECLINE, FAIR LADY! DO NOT WASTE THY LAVISH FAVORS ON ME...
FAIR LADY, THE MEMORY OF WHAT YOU'VE DONE TONIGHT WILL GO WITH ME INTO BATTLE.
...FOR I HAVE THE FAVOR... OF ANOTHER.
KISS

AND NOW...
LEAP!
...TO BATTLE!

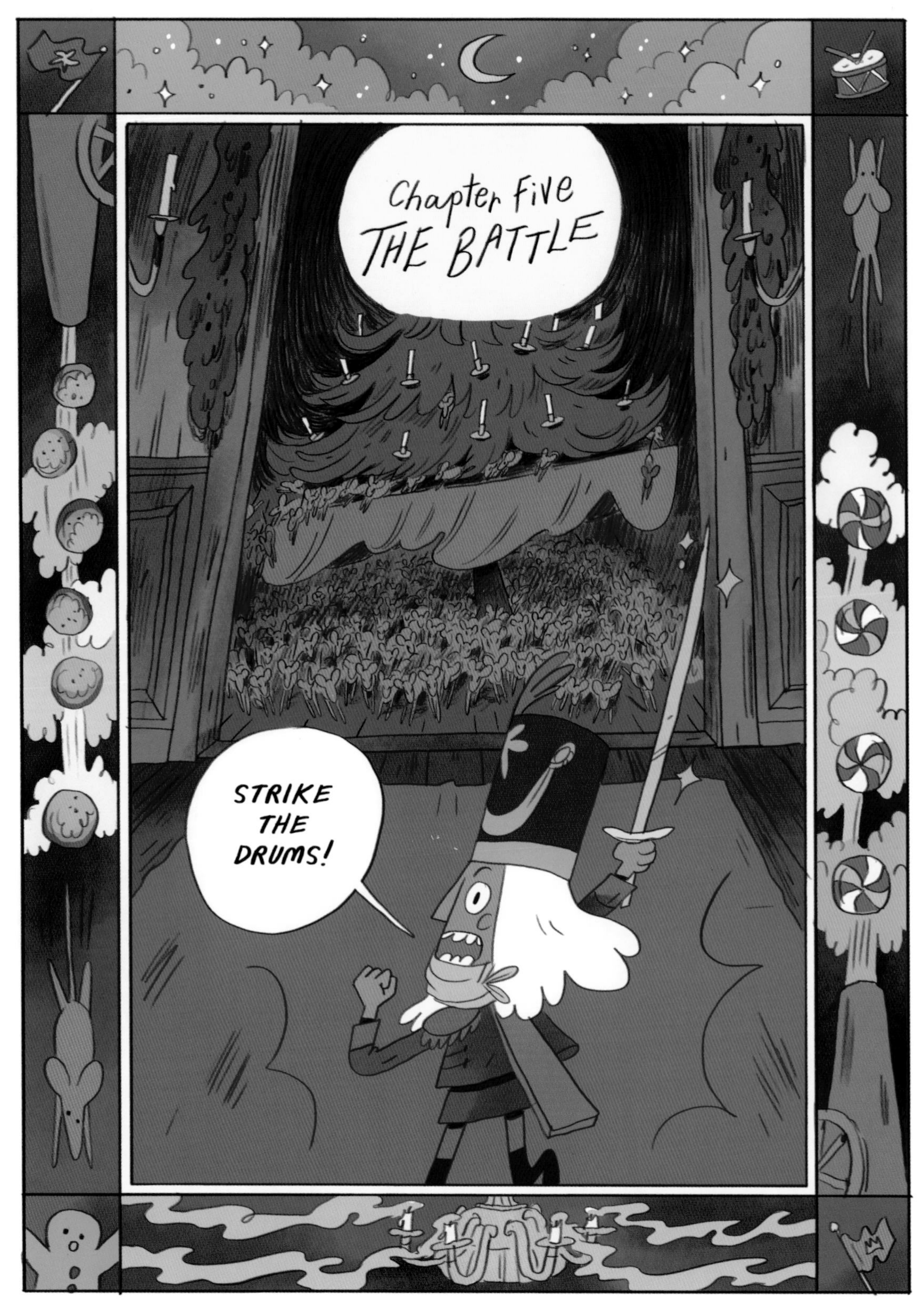
Chapter Five
THE BATTLE
STRIKE THE DRUMS!

BUM BADDA BUM
YAWN
BUM BUM BADDA BUM
LET NO MAN SLEEP!
BADDA BUM
BUM BUM
WE'LL FIGHT LIKE NEVER BEFORE! TOGETHER WE CAN DEFEAT THE MOUSE KING AND HIS EVIL MOUSE ARMY FOR GOOD!
NOW IS OUR CHANCE!
BUM BADDA-DA BUM BUM BUM BADDA-BU
AH, GENERAL! I'VE HEARD COUNTLESS TALES OF YOUR COURAGE IN BATTLE! I NEED A QUICK EYE AND THE SKILL TO SEIZE THE MOMENT AGAINST OUR ENEMIES!
BUM
BUM BADDA
BADDA
BUM
SHOONK
THEREFORE, I ENTRUST ALL THE CAVALRY TO YOUR COMMAND. I'M COUNTING ON YOU!
YES, SIR!
Fhoowewooweep!

CHARGE!
BEE BADDA BEE BEE BEE BEE BEE!
READY, SOLDIERS?!
BUM BUM BUM BADD-DA DUM BUM BUM BUM!
SQUEEAAK!!
SQUEAK!
SQUEAK!
SQUEAK!
SQUEAK!
SQUEAK!
SQUEAK!
SQUEAK!
TO WAR!!
CANNONS, FIRE!
POOF!
BOOM!
BOOM!
AHH HH!
AHH!
AHHHH!
BANG!
MARCH MARCH

POOF!
POOF!
OH! PFEFFERNUSS CANNONBALLS!
BOOM BOOM BANG
THEY'RE USING SUGARPLUMS AND PEPPERMINTS, TOO!!
SSQUEAKK!
POOF!
SHAKE
SHAKE
SHAKE
SHAKE
OH NO! THEY'RE STILL COMING!
SQUEAK!

AAAAAAHHHHHH!!!
IT'S NOW OR NEVER, SOLDIERS!
SIR, THERE ARE MORE! THEY'RE COMING FROM EVERY DIRECTION!
!!?!!!
MORE?!
AHHH!!!
COME ON, NUTCRACKER.
YOU CAN DO IT.

SQUEAK!
AHHH!!
NO!
SQUEAK!
AGHH!
SOLDIERS!!
ALL HANDS ON DECK!
BRING OUT THE RESERVES!
AH!!!
AH!!
AH!!!
AHHH!

AHHH
ARG!
RAAAAAAA!
OH MY!
YES, ONWARD!
RAAAA!
AAAA!
NO!
RETREAT!
WOO
WOO
WOO
WOO
TO THE GLASS CASE!

BACK!
HISS!
STAY BACK, YOU!
AHHHH!!
NO! WHERE ARE YOU TAKING ME?!?

NO!
TAKE YOUR PAWS OFF OF ME!
GASP!
I'VE GOT YOU NOW, NUTCRACKER!
AHHHH!
YOU WON'T BE SO PRETTY WHEN I'M DONE WITH YOU!
GASP!!
GRRRRR!
TAKE THIS, YOU MONSTER!

FOR MY NUTCRACKER!!!
SCREECH!
AAAAAAAAAAA!!
AT THAT MOMENT MARIE'S WORLD SEEMED SCATTERED AND DISPERSED.
SHE COULD FEEL THE SHOOTING PAIN IN HER LEFT ARM MUCH MORE INTENSELY THAN BEFORE.
AND SHE SANK INTO A SWOON ON THE FLOOR.

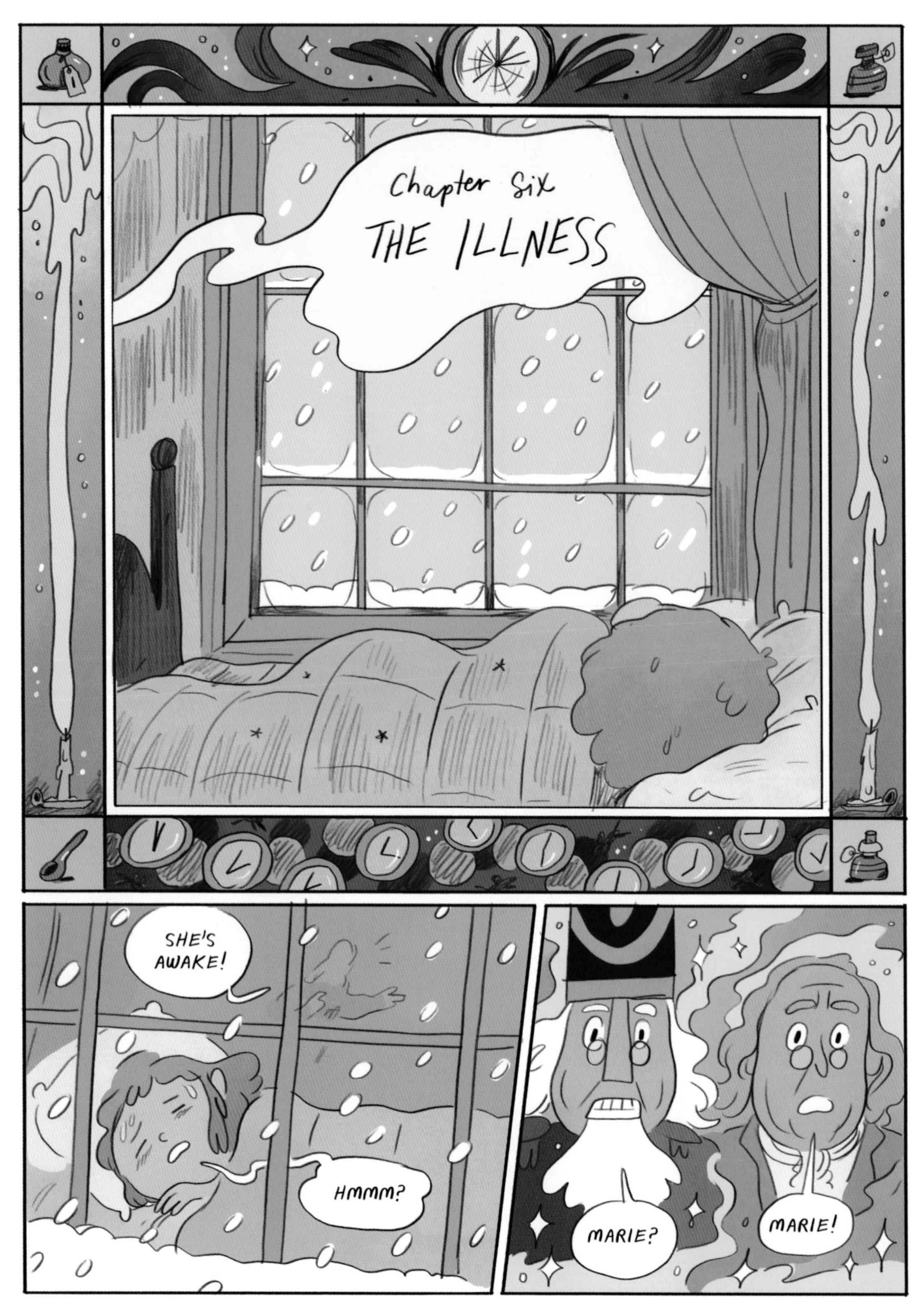
Chapter Six
THE ILLNESS
SHE'S AWAKE!
HMMM?
MARIE?
MARIE!

DOCTOR WENDELSTEIN?
YES, MARIE. YOU HAD A TERRIBLE FALL. YOU'RE LUCKY YOUR MOTHER FOUND YOU.
MARIE!
OH, MY MARIE!
OH, MOTHER, IT WAS AWFUL!
THE MOUSE KING CAME, AND HE WAS SO EVIL!
IS THE NUTCRACKER ALL RIGHT? PLEASE TELL ME HE'S NOT BROKEN INTO PIECES!
MARIE, DON'T SPEAK OF SUCH NONSENSE! WHAT DO MICE HAVE TO DO WITH NUTCRACKERS?!
PLOP!

YOU WORRIED ME SICK!
YOU DISOBEYED ME, AND LOOK WHAT HAPPENED!
YOU STAYED UP WAY TOO LATE LAST NIGHT!
YOUR NICE TOY CABINET IS RUINED!
I SEE NOW A MOUSE MUST HAVE FRIGHTENED YOU!
THAT'S THE LAST TIME I TRUST YOU TO PUT YOURSELF TO BED!
YOU CUT YOUR ARM SO BADLY THAT DOCTOR WENDELSTEIN HERE, WHO HAS JUST TAKEN GLASS SLIVERS FROM YOUR WOUND...
...THINKS IF YOU HAD CUT A VEIN YOU MIGHT HAVE BLED TO DEATH!
LUCKILY, I WOKE UP AND FOUND YOU OUT OF BED! WHEN I CHECKED DOWNSTAIRS, YOU WERE LYING ON THE FLOOR!
YOU WERE BLEEDING SO BADLY, I ALMOST FAINTED!
YOU WERE SURROUNDED BY FRITZ'S SOLDIERS, PEPPERMINTS, GINGERBREAD MEN, AND ALL YOUR FAVORITE DOLLS! DID YOU EAT SWEETS UNTIL YOU PASSED OUT AND FELL INTO THE GLASS CASE?!

I FOUND YOUR NUTCRACKER BESIDE YOU, BUT YOUR SHOE WAS ON THE OTHER SIDE OF THE ROOM!
OH, MOTHER, THOSE ARE ALL SIGNS OF THE GREAT BATTLE BETWEEN THE DOLLS AND THE MICE!
THE NUTCRACKER WAS IN GRAVE DANGER! HE COMMANDED THE ARMY THROUGH THE FIERCEST BATTLE, BUT THEN HE WAS CAPTURED BY THE MICE!
SO, YOU SEE, I HAD TO THROW MY SHOE! IN ORDER TO STOP THE MOUSE KING FROM RIPPING HIM APART!
HE HAD **SEVEN HEADS!**
ALL RIGHT, NOW. I AM SURE THERE IS AN EXPLANATION FOR ALL THIS.
THERE ARE NO MICE HERE, THE NUTCRACKER IS SAFE AND SOUND, AND THE GLASS CASE IS BEING FIXED AS WE SPEAK.
THANK YOU. I AM INDEBTED TO YOU!
IT SEEMS MARIE HAS WOUND FEVER.
POP!
OH DEAR! IS IT SERIOUS?

NOT AS LONG AS SHE STAYS IN BED FOR A FEW DAYS AND TAKES HER MEDICINE.
HOW IS MY DARLING MARIE?
KEEP AN EYE ON THIS ONE. SHE HAS QUITE THE IMAGINATION.
AH, HERR WENDELSTEIN!
HELLO, HERR DROSSELMEIER!
I CAME TO SEE FOR MYSELF HOW LITTLE MARIE IS DOING!
GODFATHER DROSSELMEIER!
YOU HAVE BEEN VERY NAUGHTY!
OH! WHAT HAVE I DONE THIS TIME?

YOU KNOW WHAT I'M TALKING ABOUT, DROSSELMEIER!
I SAW YOU UP ON THE CLOCK. YOU COVERED IT WITH YOUR COAT WINGS SO IT WOULDN'T STRIKE!! THE MICE WOULD HAVE RUN IF ONLY THE CLOCK COULD HAVE STRUCK!
AND I HEARD YOU AS YOU CALLED TO THE MOUSE KING! WHY DIDN'T YOU COME TO HELP US?! IT'S ALL **YOUR** FAULT I'M HERE, SICK IN BED!
WHAT IS THE MATTER WITH YOU, MARIE? YOUR IMAGINATION IS OUT OF CONTROL!
NO, NO. IT'S ALL RIGHT.

WATCH AS IT PURRS, PURRS...
WATCH AS THE PENDULUM WHIRS, WHIRS.
ITS BEATING BELLS BRING SLEEPING SPELLS.
WATCH AS IT PURRS, IT PURRS.
THE PENDULUM, IT TIRES OF TICKING ALL DAY...
WHIR **STRIKE** WHIR **STRIKE!**
BUT NOW IS THE TIME TO KEEP THE WRETCHED MICE AT BAY...
WHIR STRIKE WHIR STRIKE!
THE HARMONIC SWINGS HALT! AND AWAKE FROM MIDNIGHT'S VAULT...
THE OWL FLIES, SWIFT TO THE FIGHT, WINGS BEATING IN THE DEAD OF NIGHT!
THIS WAY, THAT WAY, ITS BEATING BELLS RING! BUM BUM RUM BUM, BACK IT GOES TO THE PENDULUM.

HA-HA, OH, GODFATHER DROSSELMEIER!!
YOU REMIND ME OF A DOLL OF MARIE'S I THREW BEHIND THE STOVE!
DROSSELMEIER, WHAT'S THIS ABOUT? IT'S ALL TOO STRANGE!
GRACIOUS ME! ER... YOU DON'T REMEMBER MY FAMOUS CLOCKMAKER'S RHYME?
I ALWAYS SING IT TO LIGHTEN THE SPIRITS OF THOSE AS SICK AS MARIE!
HUMPH!
PLEASE, DON'T BE ANGRY WITH ME, MARIE...
SCOOOT
I WOULD HAVE RESCUED THE NUTCRACKER, BUT THAT MOUSE KING HAD TOO MANY HEADS FOR ME TO CONTEND WITH!

HOW COULD I FACE THOSE FOURTEEN EYES ALL BY MYSELF?
HOW DO YOU KNOW ABOUT—
LISTEN, I'VE BROUGHT YOU A SURPRISE.
OH!
I'VE BEEN WORKING TO FIX HIM ALL DAY, JUST FOR YOU.
SEE, MARIE? GODFATHER DROSSELMEIER MEANS WELL BY YOUR NUTCRACKER.
YOU MUST ADMIT, THOUGH, THAT THE NUTCRACKER HAS QUITE A STRANGE BODY AND ISN'T REALLY THE NICEST DOLL. I CAN MAKE YOU SOMETHING FAR BETTER, MARIE.

YANK!
I'LL TELL YOU HOW SUCH UGLINESS FELL UPON YOUR NUTCRACKER...
...IF YOU WISH TO HEAR IT.
HE IS **NOT** UGLY. **STOP** SAYING THAT.
IF YOU HATE HOW I DESCRIBE HIM SO MUCH, PERHAPS YOU DON'T WISH TO HEAR THE STORY OF PRINCESS PIRLIPAT, THE WITCH LADY MOUSERINKS, THE ASTRONOMER, AND THE CLOCKMAKER?
AHEM, GODFATHER DROSSELMEIER, I MUST SAY...
...IT SEEMS YOU'VE FORGOTTEN SOMETHING ON THE NUTCRACKER.
??
BLASTED BOY! I DO NOT FORGET PIECES ON MY WORK!

WELL, THEN WHY DOESN'T HE HAVE A SWORD ANYMORE? WHERE DID IT GO?
OH, MUST YOU ALWAYS MEDDLE AND COMPLAIN, FRITZ?
WHY SHOULD I GIVE HIM BACK HIS SWORD? ALL HIS FIGHTING IS FINISHED. IF HE REALLY NEEDS A SWORD, HE CAN FIND ONE HIMSELF.
HMM...THAT'S TRUE. IF HE'S A TRUE SOLDIER, HE'LL BE RESOURCEFUL ENOUGH TO FIND A SWORD OR MAKE ONE ON HIS OWN.
ANYWAY, MARIE, WOULD YOU LIKE TO HEAR THE STORY OF PRINCESS PIRLIPAT?
NOD
I HOPE, DEAR COUNSELOR, THAT THIS STORY WILL NOT FRIGHTEN THEM AS YOUR STORIES OFTEN DO.
ESPECIALLY AFTER LAST NIGHT'S EVENTS.
OH NO, ON THE CONTRARY! THIS STORY WILL BE VERY, VERY BORING. IT WON'T INCLUDE ANYTHING THAT MIGHT GIVE THEM NIGHTMARES.
AT LEAST, I THINK IT WON'T...

DO TELL US, GODFATHER!
YES, PLEASE TELL US! TELL US!
HOP!
HMM, LET'S SEE... WELL, I GUESS IT STARTS LIKE THIS...
ONCE UPON A TIME...

Chapter Seven
THE KRAKATUK FAIRY TALE
ONCE UPON A TIME THERE WAS A BEAUTIFUL PRINCESS NAMED PIRLIPAT. PIRLIPAT'S MOTHER WAS A BELOVED QUEEN, AND HER FATHER WAS A GREAT AND POWERFUL KING, WHICH MADE THEIR NEWBORN BABY, PIRLIPAT, A TRUE PRINCESS.
HA-HA! HAVE YOU EVER SEEN ANYTHING MORE BEAUTIFUL THAN MY PIRLIPAT?!?
NO! NEVER, YOUR HIGHNESS!
AND IT WAS TRUE—AS LONG AS THE WORLD HAD BEEN TURNING, A LOVELIER CHILD HAD NEVER BEEN BORN.

HER FACE LOOKED LIKE IT COULD BE MADE OF LILIES AND ROSES, HER EYES SPARKLED AND GLEAMED, AND HER CHARMING LITTLE LOCKS CURLED IN BRIGHT GOLDEN RINGLETS.
BUT THE MOST INTERESTING OF HER FEATURES WAS THE FULL SET OF PEARLY WHITE TEETH SHE HAD MIRACULOUSLY BEEN BORN WITH...
ONE...
TWO...
TWENTY...
...WHICH SHE IMMEDIATELY USED TO BITE THE HIGH CHANCELLOR'S FINGER AS HE COUNTED.
YEOW!
SHAKE
SHAKE
SHAKE
THE KINGDOM TOOK IT AS A SIGN THAT SHE WOULD ONE DAY BE A FIERCE AND STRONG RULER.
AND SO EVERYONE WAS DELIGHTED BY THEIR NEW, PERFECT PRINCESS PIRLIPAT.
AGHH!
INCREDIBLE.
THE QUEEN, HOWEVER, WAS VERY ANXIOUS ABOUT LETTING PIRLIPAT OUT OF HER SIGHT. NO ONE WAS ABLE TO FIGURE OUT WHY.
EVERYONE REMARKED WITH GREAT CONCERN AT THE EXTREME MEASURES THE QUEEN TOOK TO GUARD THE CRADLE.

NOT ONLY DID SHE WATCH PIRLIPAT CLOSELY, BUT SHE ALSO HAD EVERY ENTRANCE TO THE THRONE ROOM, INCLUDING CRACKS IN THE FLOOR, GUARDED BY SOLDIERS.
SHE ALSO KEPT TWO OF HER BEST MAIDS CLOSE TO THE CRIB AT ALL TIMES, AND ENLISTED AND KEPT AN EXTRA SIX MAIDS TO SURROUND HER LIKE A FORTRESS.
BUT WHAT WAS EVEN STRANGER WAS THAT SHE HAD INSTRUCTED EACH MAID TO KEEP A CAT UPON HER LAP...
PURRR
pat pat
PURRRR
PURRRR
SCRITCH SCRITCH
...AND CONTINUOUSLY STROKE IT SO THAT IT WOULD NEVER STOP PURRING.
IT WAS IMPOSSIBLE FOR THE KINGDOM TO UNDERSTAND THE MEASURES TAKEN BY THE QUEEN...
...FOR THEY DID NOT KNOW ABOUT THE INCIDENT THAT HAD TAKEN PLACE A FEW MONTHS EARLIER.

IT HAPPENED DURING THE EVENTS LEADING UP TO A GREAT BALL...
I WANT TO SHOW THE KINGDOM THAT I WILL SPARE NO EXPENSE TO BRING THEM THE GREATEST BALL IN HISTORY!
IT SHALL BE A MASQUERADE, COMPLETE WITH THEATRICAL PERFORMANCES OF BOTH COMEDY AND TRAGEDY!
I DEMAND THERE BE A GREAT FEAST TO DISPLAY ALL THE DELICACIES OF MY LAND, FEATURING ALL OF MY MOST FAVORITE DISHES.
AH, YES, SIRE! WHAT A SPLENDID IDEA!
YES, YES, HOW STUPENDOUS, YOUR MAJESTY!

I WANT EVERYTHING TO BE PERFECT ON THIS NIGHT! WE MUST SHOW OUR NEIGHBORING KINGDOMS HOW MUCH BETTER WE ARE THAN THEM!
YOUR MAJESTY, THE COURT ASTRONOMER HAS ASSURED US THAT THE STARS ARE ALIGNED PERFECTLY FOR A LAVISH FEAST OF YOUR FAVORITE AND MOST EXPENSIVE DISH, BRATWURST WITH EXTRA FAT!
OH, WHAT A WONDERFUL PREDICTION!
MY QUEEN, YOUR SECRET BRATWURST RECIPE IS MY ABSOLUTE FAVORITE. WOULD YOU DO ME THE HONOR OF MAKING IT THE SPECIAL WAY YOU DO, WITH LOTS AND LOTS OF FAT, FOR MY GREAT BALL?
OH! I'D BE DELIGHTED, MY SWEET KING! I DO LOVE TO MAKE MY SECRET BRATWURST RECIPE, ESPECIALLY FOR YOU!

AND SO THE KING HAD THE GOLDEN SAUSAGE KETTLE, THE SILVER CHOPPING KNIVES, AND THE FINE STEW PANS ALL DELIVERED TO THE ROYAL KITCHEN FOR THE QUEEN TO COOK HER BRATWURST.
SHE REQUESTED COMPLETE PRIVACY WHILE SHE COOKED, WITH NO EXTRA MAIDS OR ROYAL CHEFS, SO SHE COULD KEEP HER RECIPE SECRET.
SLUUURP
THE QUEEN COOKED THE ENTIRE MORNING OF THE BALL BEFORE SHE REACHED THE MOST IMPORTANT PART OF HER RECIPE.
THE TIME HAD COME TO CUT THE FAT INTO CUBES AND ROAST THEM TO PERFECTION ON SILVER GRATES. AS SOON AS THE FAT BEGAN TO FRY, SHE HEARD A FAINT, WHISPERING VOICE.
GIVE ME A BIT OF THE FAT, SISTER!
I AM ALSO A QUEEN AND THEREFORE I DESERVE A PART OF THE FEAST AS WELL!
GIVE ME THE FAT!

THE QUEEN KNEW RIGHT AWAY THAT IT WAS NONE OTHER THAN THE LADY MOUSERINKS, WHO HAD LIVED IN THE PALACE KITCHENS FOR MANY YEARS, CLAIMING TO BE RELATED TO THE ROYAL FAMILY.
COME OUT, LADY MOUSERINKS!
I SHALL SHARE SOME OF MY SPECIAL RECIPE WITH YOU ON THIS FESTIVE DAY!
SIZZLE
SIZZLE
AH, THANK YOU, DEAR SISTER!
THIS WILL PLEASE MY SONS IMMENSELY!
SONS?!
SQUEAK
SQUEAK!
SQUEAK!
THE QUEEN COULD NOT REACT QUICKLY ENOUGH TO STOP LADY MOUSERINKS AND HER SEVEN SONS FROM TAKING NEARLY ALL THE FAT!
OH NO!
NOT THAT MUCH!
WITH THE HOUR OF THE FEAST RAPIDLY APPROACHING, THE QUEEN FRANTICALLY CALLED IN THE COURT MATHEMATICIAN TO SEE HOW THE SCRAPS AND CASINGS MOUSERINKS HAD LEFT BEHIND COULD BE DIVIDED AMONGST THE BRATWURST...
...BUT THE CALCULATIONS WEREN'T PROMISING.

SOON THE TIME HAD COME FOR ALL THE LORDS AND LADIES, FINE PRINCES AND PRINCESSES, AND DISTINGUISHED GUESTS FROM THROUGHOUT THE LAND TO ARRIVE FOR THE BALL.
DRUMS AND TRUMPETS ANNOUNCED THE ARRIVAL OF THE GUESTS AS THEY ENTERED THE DINING HALL FOR THE GREAT FEAST.

THE KING WELCOMED EVERYONE GRACIOUSLY TO HIS ROYAL TABLES BUT COULDN'T WAIT TO EAT.
LET THE FEAST BEGIN!
YUM!
THE KING DELIGHTED IN THE FIRST COURSE.
DELICIOUS! MY COMPLIMENTS TO THE ROYAL CHEFS!
AND THE SECOND COURSE SEEMED EVEN MORE SATISFYING.
THEN IT WAS TIME FOR THE KING'S FAVORITE COURSE...
...THE QUEEN'S SPECIAL BRATWURST WITH EXTRA FAT!
THE QUEEN LOOKED ON NERVOUSLY.
A SICKLY LOOK FELL UPON THE KING'S FACE.

OH NO!
THERE'S... TOO...LITTLE... FAT!
OH, MY POOR HUSBAND! I CANNOT GO ON KNOWING MY BRATWURST HAS UPSET YOU!
FAINT!
PLEASE REMEMBER ME FONDLY, FOR I AM NOT TO BLAME FOR THIS TRAGIC OUTCOME!
WHAT?!
WHO'S TO BLAME?!
IT WAS MOUSERINKS! YES, YES! MOUSERINKS AND HER SEVEN EVIL SONS, WHO STOLE THE FAT FROM MY STOVE AND CAUSED ALL THIS SUFFERING!
MOUSERINKS?! SEVEN EVIL SONS?!
YES! IT WAS ALL THEIR FAULT! YOU MUST PUNISH THEM FOR THEIR CRIMES! IN THE NAME OF THE BRATWURST!
I WILL HAVE REVENGE UPON THE MOUSERINKS FAMILY FOR STEALING FROM THE ROYAL COURT AND UPSETTING THE QUEEN!
THEY WILL PAY FOR RUINING MY FAVORITE MEAL AND SPOILING MY BALL!
SLAM!
LADY MOUSERINKS WAS SUMMONED TO THE HIGH COURT, WHERE THE JUDGE SEIZED ALL HER ESTATES UNDER THE VARIOUS ROYAL STOVES. THE JUDGES FORCED HER TO MOVE HER FAMILY UNDER THE CASTLE FLOORBOARDS— A HUMILIATING SENTENCE FOR MOUSERINKS.
YET THE KING WAS AFRAID THAT MOUSERINKS IN TURN MIGHT WANT REVENGE FOR THE LOSS OF HER ANCESTRAL HOME. SO HE DECIDED TO TAKE MATTERS INTO HIS OWN HANDS.
HMM...

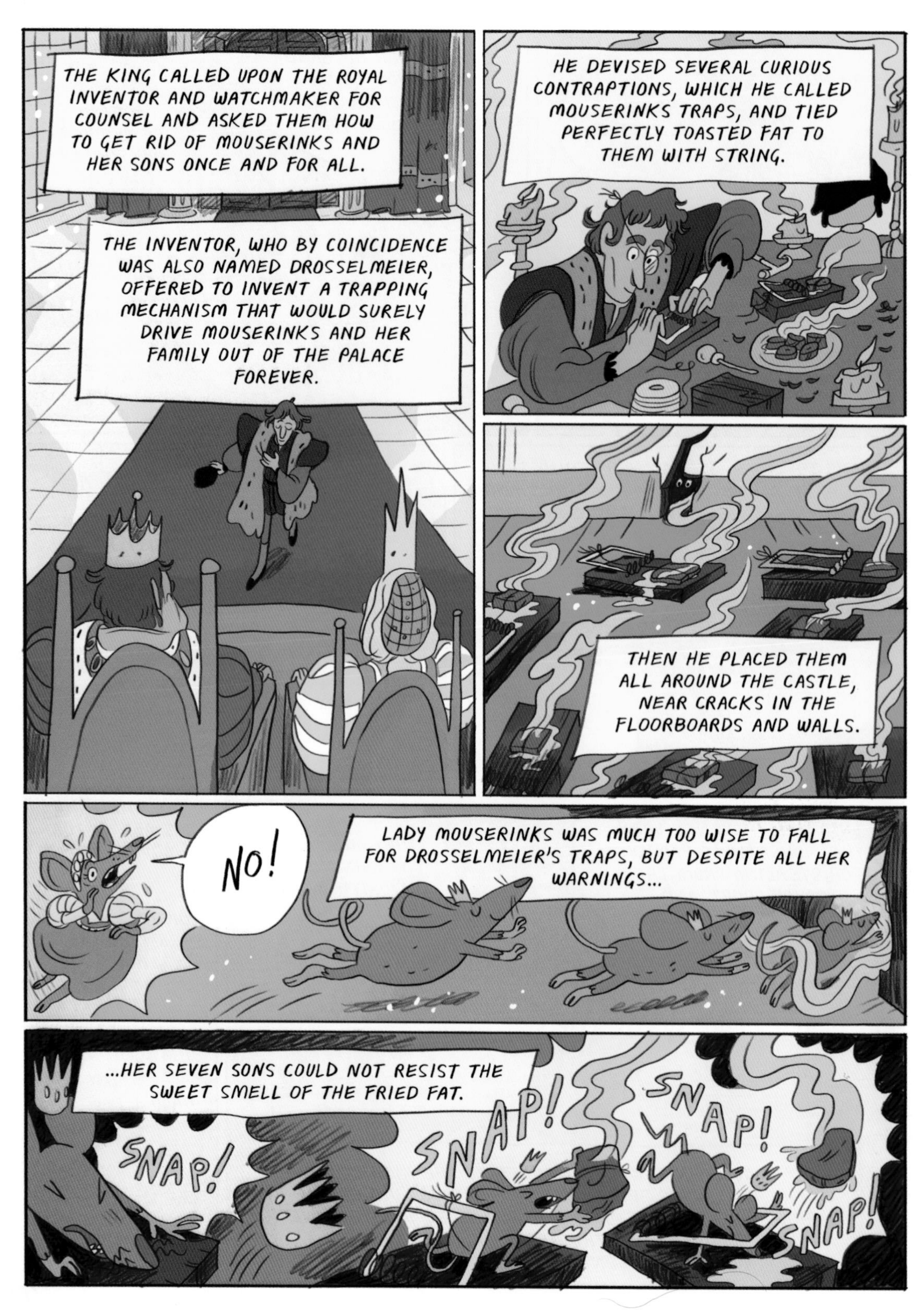
THE KING CALLED UPON THE ROYAL INVENTOR AND WATCHMAKER FOR COUNSEL AND ASKED THEM HOW TO GET RID OF MOUSERINKS AND HER SONS ONCE AND FOR ALL.
THE INVENTOR, WHO BY COINCIDENCE WAS ALSO NAMED DROSSELMEIER, OFFERED TO INVENT A TRAPPING MECHANISM THAT WOULD SURELY DRIVE MOUSERINKS AND HER FAMILY OUT OF THE PALACE FOREVER.
HE DEVISED SEVERAL CURIOUS CONTRAPTIONS, WHICH HE CALLED MOUSERINKS TRAPS, AND TIED PERFECTLY TOASTED FAT TO THEM WITH STRING.
THEN HE PLACED THEM ALL AROUND THE CASTLE, NEAR CRACKS IN THE FLOORBOARDS AND WALLS.
NO!
LADY MOUSERINKS WAS MUCH TOO WISE TO FALL FOR DROSSELMEIER'S TRAPS, BUT DESPITE ALL HER WARNINGS...
...HER SEVEN SONS COULD NOT RESIST THE SWEET SMELL OF THE FRIED FAT.
SNAP!
SNAP!
SNAP!
SNAP!

AFTERWARD, LADY MOUSERINKS LEFT THE CASTLE IN DESPAIR, CARRYING ONLY HER SONS' SEVEN CROWNS—ALL THAT WAS LEFT OF HER ROYAL FAMILY.
KRACK
GRIEF AND REVENGE FILLED HER HEART.
TINK
TINK
TINK
BURRRRRR
BURRRRRR
THE COURT REJOICED AS MOUSERINKS FLED, BUT THE QUEEN WAS ANXIOUS. SHE REGRETTED TELLING THE KING ABOUT THE STOLEN FAT.
BURRRURRRRR
JUST THE NIGHT BEFORE, LADY MOUSERINKS HAD VISITED THE QUEEN'S BEDSIDE AND WHISPERED IN HER EAR...
MY SONS, MY FAMILY, MY ENTIRE BLOODLINE—DESTROYED! ALL OVER SOME MEASLY BRATWURST FAT!
TAKE CARE, MY QUEEN, THAT I DO NOT BITE YOUR FUTURE SONS OR DAUGHTERS AND TAKE REVENGE ON YOUR BLOODLINE! TAKE VERY GOOD CARE...
THE QUEEN WATCHED AS MOUSERINKS LEFT THE KINGDOM...
...AND KNEW THAT SOMEDAY SHE WOULD RETURN.
BURRRRR
BURRRRR

AND THAT'S ENOUGH FOR THIS EVENING, CHILDREN.
CRRAACK!!
AW!!
WHY MUST WE STOP?!
TOO MUCH IS UNHEALTHY FOR ONE NIGHT! BUT HAVE NO FEAR. I'LL CONTINUE TOMORROW.
GODFATHER, IS IT TRUE YOU INVENTED THE MOUSETRAP?
HOW CAN YOU ASK SUCH A SILLY QUESTION, MARIE?! HE OBVIOUSLY DIDN'T ACTUALLY INVENT IT.
AM I NOT A SKILLFUL CLOCKMAKER? WHY SHOULD IT BE SO SILLY TO THINK THAT I MIGHT HAVE INVENTED SUCH A DEVICE? HMM?
KEEP IN MIND YOU DON'T KNOW EVERYTHING, YOUNG FRITZ.
COME NOW, TIME FOR BED.
HUMPH!
GRRR...

THAT EVENING, AFTER THE STAHLBAUM FAMILY HAD GONE TO SLEEP, MARIE HEARD SOMETHING STRANGE.
TICK TOCK TICK TOCK
ALWAYS WATCHING BY THE CLOCK,
WE HUNT FOR SOMETHING WE WILL LIKE...
THE MICE...
BUT HAVE TO WAIT FOR MIDNIGHT'S STRIKE!
GIVE US, GIVE US WHAT WE DESIRE, SO WE CAN EAT IT BY THE FIRE.
IT MUST BE SOMETHING YOU LOVE MOST, OR NUTCRACKER'S FACE INSTEAD WE'LL ROAST!
SILLY GIRL, YOUR SHOE CAN'T DEFEAT ME! I WON'T GO AWAY SO EASILY. TONIGHT YOU'LL BRING ME ALL YOUR SWEETS— I WANT TO FEAST ON YOUR CHRISTMAS TREATS! LEAVE THEM LOW AND IN PLAIN SIGHT...
...OR I'LL GNAW ON NUTCRACKER'S FACE TONIGHT!
DON'T WAIT, SILLY GIRL! DON'T YOU BE LATE!
TELL A SOUL, AND SEAL NUTCRACKER'S FATE!

OH DEAR, OH DEAR, OH DEAR!
OH, IF ONLY I COULD WAKE UP MOTHER AND FATHER!
EVEN IF I COULD TELL THEM, THEY WOULD NEVER BELIEVE ME.
THEY WOULD JUST LAUGH AT ME AND TELL ME IT'S BECAUSE I'M SICK!
WELL, IT'S UP TO ME, THEN. IT'S EITHER THE NUTCRACKER OR MY SUGARPLUMS AND MARZIPAN.
AND IT'LL ALWAYS BE MY NUTCRACKER.

THE NEXT MORNING MARIE'S FATHER CAME INTO HER ROOM WITH HIS HEAD HUNG LOW.
OH, MARIE. I'M SO SORRY, BUT IT SEEMS SOME MICE HAVE GOTTEN INTO ALL YOUR SWEETS AND RUINED THEM.
IT DOESN'T LOOK LIKE THE MICE LIKED THE SWEETS, THOUGH...
...BECAUSE THEY WERE NOT COMPLETELY EATEN! SEE? I WANTED TO LET YOU KNOW THAT WHAT'S LEFT WILL HAVE TO BE THROWN AWAY.
BUT, MARIE, HOW DID YOUR CANDY BOWL END UP DOWNSTAIRS?
IT WORKED!
MARIE? WHAT WORKED?
MARIE, ARE YOU LISTENING TO ME?
MARIE WAS NOT LISTENING TO HER FATHER. ALL SHE COULD THINK ABOUT WAS HOW SHE HAD SAVED THE NUTCRACKER FROM THE FATE OF HER CHRISTMAS CANDIES.
WHAT HAS GOTTEN INTO YOU, MARIE?
AH, EVERYONE'S HERE! SHALL WE CONTINUE THE STORY OF PRINCESS PIRLIPAT AND THE VENGEFUL MOUSERINKS?
YES!
AH, YES. RIGHT ON TIME, DROSSELMEIER.

Chapter Eight
THE FAIRY TALE CONTINUED
SO NOW YOU KNOW WHY THE QUEEN WAS SO CAUTIOUS AND WHY SHE KEPT PIRLIPAT GUARDED AT ALL TIMES.
SHE WAS RIGHTFULLY AFRAID THAT LADY MOUSERINKS WOULD HAVE HER REVENGE ON THE PRINCESS.
IN FACT, WHEN THE QUEEN FOUND OUT SHE WAS PREGNANT WITH PRINCESS PIRLIPAT, SHE FEARED DROSSELMEIER'S TRAPPING MACHINES WOULD BE NO MATCH FOR MOUSERINKS'S WIT AND FURY.
SO SHE DECIDED TO CONSULT THE COURT ASTRONOMER FOR ADVICE ON KEEPING MOUSERINKS AWAY.
YES, YES!
CRASH!
KNOCK KNOCK
BOOM!
COMING!

MY QUEEN?
I NEED YOUR HELP.
AFTER THE QUEEN EXPLAINED HER HISTORY WITH MOUSERINKS, THE ASTRONOMER BEGAN HIS STAR READINGS AND HOROSCOPE WRITING.
HE READ THAT KEEPING CATS PURRING AROUND THE PRINCESS ALL DAY AND ALL NIGHT WOULD KEEP MOUSERINKS AWAY. AND SO SHE DID AS HE INSTRUCTED.
THE CATS SEEMED TO BE WORKING WELL, UNTIL ONE FATEFUL NIGHT...
ALL THE MAIDS, NURSES, GUARDS, AND CATS FELL ASLEEP QUITE SUDDENLY AT THE STROKE OF MIDNIGHT.
PITTER PATTER PITTER
YAWN
THE SOUND OF LITTLE FEET FILLED THE ROOM AND STIRRED ONE OF THE MAIDS FROM HER DEEP SLUMBER.
SHE JUMPED UP WHEN SHE NOTICED EVERYONE AROUND HER WAS ASLEEP!
AND THEN SHE SAW...
...MOUSERINKS!!!

BITE!
MOUSERINKS BIT THE PRINCESS ON HER HEAD!
HUMPH!
BOUNCE
AND SHE LEAPT AWAY!
WAAAAAAAA!
WAAAAA!
GUARDS!!!
WAAAAA WAAAAAAAAAA!
WAAAA!
THE GUARDS AWOKE AND SCRAMBLED TO CATCH LADY MOUSERINKS—BUT SHE WAS MUCH TOO QUICK AND SMALL FOR THEM!
SHE SLIPPED INTO A CRACK IN THE WALL...
SLIP!
...AND ESCAPED.
AHH!!!!!
WAAAA
WAAAAAA!
OH NO! NOT MY PIRLIPAT!
SOMETHING STRANGE WAS HAPPENING TO PIRLIPAT.

HER HEAD BEGAN TO GROW TWICE THE SIZE OF HER LITTLE BODY, AND SEVERAL WHITE HAIRS POPPED OUT FROM HER CHIN.
HER BLUE EYES BEGAN PROTRUDING OUT OF HER HEAD AND HER SWEET LITTLE MOUTH BECAME A LARGE, TWISTED SMILE.
THE KING RUSHED IN.
MOUSERINKS DID IT!
NO!
WAAAAAAAA!
OH, WHY DID I CARE SO MUCH ABOUT MY BRATWURST?!
WHY DIDN'T I JUST LEAVE MOUSERINKS AND HER WHOLE EVIL FAMILY UNDER THE STOVES?!
THE KING SUMMONED THE COURT INVENTOR AND DEMANDED HE FIND A WAY TO RETURN THE PRINCESS TO HER FORMER BEAUTY.
WAAAH!
WAHH!
WAHH!
I'LL CALL UPON THE COURT EXECUTIONER IF YOU FAIL!
GULP!
DROSSELMEIER STUDIED PIRLIPAT, SEEKING A SOLUTION.
WAAA!
WAAAA!
WAAAA!
WAAA!
MUNCH MUNCH
HE STARTED EATING WALNUTS TO CONCENTRATE THROUGH ALL HER SCREAMING.
PIRLIPAT SUDDENLY QUIETED.
Eeeeeee!!!
??
DO YOU WANT A WALNUT, PIRLIPAT?

Eeeeeeeeee!!!
NOD
NOD
NOD
NOD
CRACK!
AS SOON AS SHE BIT INTO THE WALNUT'S SHELL WITH HER SHARP TEETH, PIRLIPAT BECAME HAPPY AGAIN.
DROSSELMEIER TOOK THIS AS A CLUE.
I MUST MEET WITH THE COURT ASTRONOMER ABOUT THIS AT ONCE!
THE KING GRANTED DROSSELMEIER AN AUDIENCE WITH THE COURT ASTRONOMER, THOUGH HE WAS KEPT UNDER HEAVY GUARD IN CASE HE TRIED TO FLEE.
WHEN THEY SAW EACH OTHER, THE TWO MEN EMBRACED IN TEARS. FOR THE MAN DROSSELMEIER SOUGHT FOR COUNSEL WAS NOT ONLY A FELLOW MEMBER OF THE ROYAL COURT BUT HIS DEAR OLDER BROTHER AS WELL.
LITTLE BROTHER! SO GOOD TO SEE YOU!
AH, DEAR BROTHER! I'M SO SORRY TO BE COMING TO YOU UNDER THESE CIRCUMSTANCES.
THEY DISCUSSED PRINCESS PIRLIPAT'S CONDITION AND BEGAN THEIR RESEARCH.
THEY STARTED IN THE ASTRONOMER'S LIBRARY AND SCOURED ALL HIS ANCIENT BOOKS ON HOROSCOPES INVOLVING MICE, NUTS, AND EVIL SPELLS.
OOMF
BUT AFTER HOURS, THEY FOUND NOTHING.
HMM...WHAT IF WE REMAKE PIRLIPAT'S HOROSCOPE? BUT THIS TIME FOLLOW ALL THE LINES.

REMAKING PRINCESS PIRLIPAT'S HOROSCOPE PROVED TO BE A GREAT DEAL MORE TROUBLE THAN THE ASTRONOMER EXPECTED. AS HE AND DROSSELMEIER DREW THE LINES FOR HER PLANETS AND MOONS, THE PATHS GREW MORE AND MORE INTRICATE, WITH MANY MORE ALIGNMENTS THAN THE ASTRONOMER HAD EVER ENCOUNTERED.

BUT AFTER LONG HOURS OF STARING AT THE NIGHT SKY, IT BECAME CLEAR TO THEM WHAT HAD TO BE DONE IN ORDER TO FREE PIRLIPAT FROM THE MAGIC THAT HAD TRANSFORMED HER.

THE ASTRONOMER READ THAT SHE WOULD HAVE TO EAT THE SWEET KERNEL OF THE RARE KRAKATUK NUT AND THAT IT MUST BE BOTH CRACKED OPEN AND PRESENTED TO HER BY A BOY.

THE BOY HAD TO HAVE NEVER WORN BOOTS OR GROWN A WHISKER, SO HE'D NEED TO BE QUITE YOUNG. HE MUST ALSO HAVE IMPECCABLE BALANCE, FOR HE WOULD HAVE TO WALK SEVEN STEPS BACKWARD WITH HIS EYES SHUT AFTER GIVING THE PRINCESS THE KRAKATUK.

THIS SEEMED DIFFICULT BUT STILL POSSIBLE...UNTIL THEY READ THAT THE KRAKATUK WAS THE RAREST NUT IN THE WORLD, AND ALSO THE HARDEST.

FINDING A BOY TO CRACK IT WOULD BE IMPOSSIBLE, EVEN IF THEY DID EVER **FIND** THE NUT.

THE COURT INVENTOR AND THE ROYAL ASTRONOMER EXPLAINED WHAT WOULD HAVE TO BE DONE TO TURN THE PRINCESS PIRLIPAT BACK INTO HER FORMER SELF.
HMM...BUT WHERE WILL YOU FIND THIS KRAKATUK?
WE'LL START OUR JOURNEY TO FIND IT RIGHT AWAY, YOUR HIGHNESS!
WE WILL?
THE BOTH OF US?
WELL, THEN! THIS SOUNDS LIKE A GREAT IDEA! HA-HA! I'LL EVEN MAKE THIS BOY A PRINCE WHEN HE GIVES MY PIRLIPAT THE RARE KRAKATUK!
BUT...
...IF THIS BOY FAILS, OR YOU COME BACK EMPTY-HANDED... I'LL HAVE YOU BOTH EXECUTED!
DO I MAKE MYSELF CLEAR?
THE NEXT DAY THE ASTRONOMER VISITED HIS HOME IN THE COUNTRY BEFORE SETTING OFF TO FIND THE KRAKATUK. HIS WIFE, WHO RESIDED IN THEIR COTTAGE WHILE THE ASTRONOMER WORKED IN THE CASTLE TOWERS, SOLEMNLY BID THEM BOTH FAREWELL.
BUT BEFORE SHE SAID HER FINAL GOOD-BYES, SHE VOWED TO DO EVERYTHING IN HER POWER TO LOOK FOR SIGNS OF THE KRAKATUK AND THE BOY IN THE KINGDOM WHILE THE BROTHERS SEARCHED ABROAD.

AND THAT IS ALL FOR NOW, CHILDREN.
NO, IT'S JUST GETTING GOOD! AN EPIC ADVENTURE! I CAN'T WAIT!
PERHAPS DREAMS OF ADVENTURE AWAIT YOU IN TONIGHT'S SLEEP? YOU NEVER KNOW!
COME NOW, FRITZ, I PROMISE TO CONTINUE TOMORROW. FOR THE MOMENT, WE MUST LET MARIE SLEEP.
BUT MARIE SLEPT VERY LITTLE THAT NIGHT, FOR THE MOUSE KING SOON ARRIVED AGAIN WITH ANOTHER REQUEST.
AH-HA! I ENJOYED THE FEAST YOU LEFT IN THE HALL,
AND TONIGHT I WANT ALL YOUR MOST BEAUTIFUL DOLLS!
GULP!
LEAVE THEM FOR ME IN THE EXACT SAME SPOT, OR NUTCRACKER'S WOODEN HEAD WILL ROT!
I WON'T WAIT LONG...
...SO DON'T DELAY!
OR MORNING WILL COME WITH CRIES OF DISMAY!

MARIE, VERY DISTRESSED, RAN DOWNSTAIRS TO TAKE HER DOLLS OUT OF THE GLASS CABINET.
SHE DIDN'T CARE MUCH FOR MADAME D'ORLEANS OR THE SHEPHERDESS WITH HER LITTLE LAMBS, SO SHE DIDN'T MIND PUTTING THOSE DOLLS OUT FOR THE MOUSE KING.
BUT SHE HESITATED WHEN SHE PICKED UP MISS CLARETTE. WOULD THE MOUSE KING CONSIDER HER ONE OF MARIE'S MOST BEAUTIFUL DOLLS? SHE'D ALREADY BEEN PLAYED WITH SO MUCH...
SHE DECIDED MISS CLARETTE DIDN'T COUNT AND PUT OUT THE LESS PLAYED WITH, MORE PRISTINE DOLLS INSTEAD.
SHE KISSED EACH ONE AS SHE LAID THEM OUT FOR THE MOUSE KING, THEN WENT BACK UPSTAIRS TO SLEEP.
OH, NUTCRACKER...
...WHAT WOULD I NOT DO TO SAVE YOU FROM THE VILE MOUSE KING?
I HOPE THIS IS THE END OF THE MOUSE KING'S TORMENT AND YOU CAN LIVE IN PEACE ONCE MORE.

Chapter Nine
THE FAIRY TALE FINALE

I'M SO SORRY, DEAR. THERE MUST BE AN AWFULLY BIG MOUSE IN THE HOUSE...
...BECAUSE THIS MORNING I FOUND ALL YOUR NEW, EXPENSIVE DOLLS BITTEN AND TORN.
BUT I DONT UNDERSTAND, MARIE—WHY WERE ALL YOUR DOLLS LEFT OUT IN THE FIRST PLACE?
MARIE KNEW SHE'D SAVED THE NUTCRACKER YET AGAIN AND TRIED NOT TO THINK ABOUT HER TORN DOLLS.
MARIE? DID YOU HEAR WHAT I SAID?
MARIE, THIS IS VERY ODD. WE'LL HAVE TO LOCK UP ALL YOUR DOLLS IF THIS CONTINUES.
I COULD BUILD A MOUSETRAP TO LAY OUT TONIGHT, MRS. STAHLBAUM. PERHAPS WE COULD CATCH THIS MOUSE FOR GOOD?
WELL, THEN, GODFATHER, IT MUST BE YOUR BEST WORK!
YES, FRITZ, EACH PIECE I COMPLETE IS MY BEST, I ASSURE YOU.
YES, BUT IT MUST BE ESPECIALLY GOOD THIS TIME! SINCE YOU ARE, AFTER ALL, THE INVENTOR OF THE MOUSETRAP!
THERE'S NO ROOM FOR ERROR HERE!
YES, IT'S TRUE!
YOU MUST SEE TO IT THAT THIS IS YOUR BEST WORK! THE MOUSE KING IS VERY CLEVER. HE MAY WELL COME FOR **YOU** IF HE ESCAPES YOUR TRAP!
OH DEAR...
LET'S JUST CONTINUE THE STORY, SHALL WE?

WE BEGIN AGAIN WITH THE ASTRONOMER AND THE INVENTOR ON THEIR JOURNEY FOR THE RARE KRAKATUK NUT AND THE SPECIAL BOY WHO COULD CRACK IT.
THEY SAILED ACROSS EVERY OCEAN, SPEAKING TO SAILORS AND THEIR CAPTAINS. THEY TREKKED ACROSS EVERY DESERT, INQUIRING AMONG MERCHANTS AND THEIR TRADESMEN. AND THEY CLIMBED NEARLY EVERY MOUNTAIN, VISITING WITH ANY MONK WHO WOULD SIT WITH THEM. ALL WITHOUT A TRACE OF THE RARE KRAKATUK NUT.
EACH TIME THEY FOUND A CLUE, THEIR LEADS WOULD PROVE FRUITLESS, AND SOON THEY BEGAN TO LOSE HOPE...ESPECIALLY IN EVER FINDING THE BOY, WHO NO ONE BELIEVED COULD POSSIBLY EXIST.
YEAR AFTER YEAR THEY GREW MORE HOPELESS, AND YEAR AFTER YEAR THEY FELT A DEEPER DESIRE TO RETURN HOME.
ONE NIGHT, AS THEY SMOKED THEIR PIPES IN THE MIDDLE OF A GIANT FOREST ACROSS THE WORLD FROM THEIR KINGDOM, THEIR LONGING FOR HOME BECAME TOO HEAVY TO BEAR.

BROTHER, WE'VE HAD NO SIGN OF THE KRAKATUK OR THE BOY FOR TEN YEARS. I SAY WE RETURN HOME.
YOU KNOW WE CAN'T.
I MISS MY HOME! I WANT TO SEE MY WIFE! IT'S BEEN TOO LONG! I WANT TO GO BACK!
BUT WE'LL BE EXECUTED IF WE RETURN EMPTY-HANDED. THE KING MADE HIMSELF VERY CLEAR.
WE'LL BE SEARCHING UNTIL WE'VE WASTED OUR LIVES AWAY! WHAT IF THE NUT DOESN'T EXIST?! WHAT IF WE NEVER FIND THE BOY?! WHAT IF THEY'VE TURNED PIRLIPAT BACK ALREADY AND WE DON'T EVEN KNOW?!
POHF POHF
POHF
HMM...I SUPPOSE IT HAS BEEN TEN YEARS.
I MUST AGREE. WE'VE HEARD NOTHING. LET'S GO HOME JUST TO SEE.
SO THEY STOOD UP RIGHT THEN AND THERE, PUT OUT THEIR PIPES, PACKED UP THEIR THINGS...
...AND CHARTED A COURSE BACK HOME.
THEY TOOK THE FASTEST ROUTE POSSIBLE...
...AND MADE IT HOME AT LONG LAST.

THE ASTRONOMER BROKE INTO A RUN WHEN HE SAW HIS OLD HOME. IT LOOKED EXACTLY HOW HE HAD LEFT IT, EXCEPT FOR ONE THING...
CRUNCH!
KEEP PRACTICING!
THERE WAS A SMALL BOY IN THE YARD WHOM HE HADN'T SEEN BEFORE. HE LOOKED ODDLY FAMILIAR, THOUGH.
HELLO?
?
CRUNCH
MUNCH
MUNCH
MUNCH
HUH?
WHO'S THIS?
CRASH!
GASP!
I THOUGHT YOU WERE DEAD!
HA-HA! I'M NOT DEAD! OR...NOT YET, AT LEAST!
WE'VE RETURNED HOME EMPTY-HANDED. WE DID NOT FIND THE KRAKATUK OR THE BOY!
THE KING WILL EXECUTE US WHEN HE FINDS OUT.
WE MUST THINK UP SOMETHING... AND QUICK!
I THINK I HAVE JUST THE SOLUTION!
BUT FIRST...

I'D LIKE TO INTRODUCE YOU TO YOUR SON!
WE'VE BEEN PRACTICING CRACKING A KRAKATUK NUT FOR THE TEN YEARS SINCE YOU LEFT.
HE'S VERY GOOD! HE'S LEARNED ALL ABOUT THE PROPHECY SINCE HE WAS BORN. HE MAY BE JUST THE BOY YOU NEED!
...
THAT'S INCREDIBLE!
I HAVE A SON!! WOW! NOW ALL WE NEED IS TO FIND THE KRAKATUK!
ON THAT MATTER, I HAVE SOMETHING THAT MIGHT BE OF INTEREST TO YOU...
I BOUGHT THIS BEAUTIFUL BOX FROM AN ODD VENDOR AT THE MARKET.
WHEN I LOOKED INSIDE AND FOUND A STRANGE-LOOKING NUT, I TRIED TO ASK THE SELLER ABOUT IT— BUT THEY HAD DISAPPEARED!
I'VE KEPT IT FOR YEARS JUST IN CASE IT WAS THE KRAKATUK!
IS THIS WHAT YOU'VE BEEN LOOKING FOR?
THE KRAKATUK?!!!
THIS IS UNBELIEVABLE! YOUR SON IS THE PERFECT AGE! THAT IS THE KRAKATUK! WE MUST GO TO THE KING AT ONCE BEFORE HE HEARS OF OUR RETURN AND SENDS HIS SOLDIERS FOR US!
MY SON...
...COULD YOU...
...DO YOU THINK YOU'RE READY TO FULFILL THE PROPHECY?
NOD NOD
YES!

GOOD LUCK!
DO YOU KNOW ALL THE STEPS?
I THINK SO!
JUST BITE THE KRAKATUK OPEN, PRESENT THE KERNEL TO THE PRINCESS, AND CLOSE YOUR EYES.
THEN, WHILE KEEPING YOUR EYES SHUT, WALK BACKWARD SEVEN STEPS. ON THE SEVENTH STEP THE CURSE WILL BE LIFTED!
ASTRONOMER! INVENTOR! YOU TWO HAVE BEEN GONE FOR FAR TOO LONG. YOU'D BETTER HAVE WHAT YOU NEED TO BREAK MOUSERINKS'S SPELL! OR ELSE!
YES, YOUR HIGHNESS, WE HAVE THE KRAKATUK!
GULP
AS WELL AS THE BOY NUTCRACKER, MY NEPHEW, WHO WILL PRESENT IT TO HER.
EXCELLENT! MY OFFER STILL STANDS...PIRLIPAT WILL MAKE HIM HER PRINCE IF HE SUCCEEDS!
HAVE HIM PROCEED WITH THE KRAKATUK CEREMONY IMMEDIATELY!

OKAY. YOU KNOW WHAT TO DO.
OH, HE'S SUCH A HANDSOME BOY! I WOULD LOVE TO MAKE HIM MY PRINCE. THAT'S WHAT I WANT MOST OF ALL!
YES DARLING. ANYTHING FOR YOU, PRINCESS.
SILENCE, SILENCE IN THE COURT! LET THE KRAKATUK NUTCRACKER PROCEED!
CLAP CLAP CLAP
GASP!
WOW!
GASP!
OH!!
GASP
GASP!
HMM...
I CAN DO THIS.
CRAAAACK!
CRAAAAACK!
CRAAACK!
PEW
OH! LOOK! HE'S SUCH A GOOD NUTCRACKER!
I'M VERY IMPRESSED! YOU'RE ALMOST AS GOOD AS ME!
HERE YOU ARE, YOUR HIGHNESS.

NOW...JUST A FEW STEPS FARTHER...
IT LOOKS LIKE IT'S GOING TO WORK!
I CAN'T BELIEVE IT! LOOK, SHE'S TRANSFORMING!
MUNCH
MUNCH
MUNCH
ONE...TWO...
...THREE...FOUR...
...FIVE... SIX...
THE NUTCRACKER DID IT! PIRLIPAT HAS RETURNED TO HER FORMER BEAUTY!
OH, MY SWEET PIRLIPAT! I'M GOING TO GIVE THE NEW PRINCE MY CROWN—I'M SO HAPPY!
BUT THERE'S ONE MORE STEP!
GASP! GASP!
GASP! GASP!
WAIT—WHAT'S THAT?! OH NO!

MOUSERINKS CAME BOLTING FROM THE SHADOWS, CURSING REVENGE SPELLS AS SHE RAN!
Squeak!
Squeak!
Squeak!
Squeak!
Squeak!
Squeak!
Squeak!
Squeak!
JUST AS THE ASTRONOMER'S SON WAS TAKING HIS LAST STEP, MOUSERINKS LEAPT UNDER HIS SHOE SO HE COULD NOT COMPLETE IT.
WHOOOA
WHOAA
...SEVEN... OH!!!
Squeak!
GASP!
OH NO!
SSSSSLIIIIPPPPPPP!!
GASP!
GASP!
GASP!
HE LOST HIS FOOTING AND FELL BACKWARD WITH A LOUD, WOODEN THUD.
SCREAMS FILLED THE ROYAL HALL.
Auuuhgghhh
squeaaKkkkk
NO!!
MOUSERINKS HAD INTERFERED WITH THE CEREMONY. THE LAST STEP WAS NEVER TAKEN, AND IT SEEMED THAT, HAVING FAILED IN HIS TASK, THE NUTCRACKER HAD BECOME WHAT PIRLIPAT HAD ONCE BEEN.

OH NO!
MY SON!
OH, KRAKATUK! I SHOULD HAVE KNOWN THERE WAS A WEAKNESS IN MY SPELL!
NOW MY REVENGE IS PASSED ON TO THE ONE WHO BROKE IT—THE NUTCRACKER WHO GAVE HAPPINESS TO MY ENEMIES!
BY MY SONS' SEVEN CROWNS, MY FAMILY—MY KINGDOM—WILL BE AVENGED! THOUGH I DIE, THIS NUTCRACKER WILL PAY!
YUCK!
WHAT IS THAT THING?!?
THAT'S NOT MY PRINCE! I'VE BEEN TRICKED!
TAKE IT AWAY FROM MY SIGHT! THROW THE NUTCRACKER AND HIS FAMILY IN THE DUNGEONS!
NO! PLEASE!
I'M SORRY, SON.
WE HAVE TO GO!
GUARDS! YOU HEARD HER! DUNGEONS!
SEIZE THEM!
RUN!

THEY FLED TO THE ASTRONOMER'S HOME BUT KNEW THEY COULDN'T STAY IN THE KINGDOM LONG.
WE DON'T HAVE MUCH TIME.
FIRST I MUST LOOK AT MY SON'S HOROSCOPES! THERE MUST BE A WAY TO REVERSE THIS!
GASP!
WHAT HAPPENED?!
WELL...
...I DIDN'T DO IT RIGHT... AND I DON'T KNOW WHAT HAPPENED...
...AND THEN MOUSERINKS CURSED ME... AND...NOW MY CHIN IS ITCHY.
MOUSERINKS?!?!
LOOK! I FOUND SOMETHING! THIS ISN'T PERMANENT!

IT SAYS HE CAN STILL BECOME A PRINCE! AND EVEN A KING, DESPITE THE CURSE!
BUT HE WON'T RETURN TO HIS OLD SELF UNTIL HE DEFEATS THE SON OF MOUSERINKS...
GULP
SHE'S MADE A NEW SON, BORN OUT OF THE SEVEN CROWNS OF HER PREVIOUS SONS...AND HE NOW CONTROLS THE KINGDOM OF MICE.
THERE'S MORE! HE MUST ALSO MEET SOMEONE NEW WHO WILL LOVE HIM WITH ALL THEIR HEART...
...AND PROVE THAT THEY ARE LOYAL TO HIM NO MATTER WHAT.
ALL RIGHT, THAT'S ALL FOR TONIGHT, CHILDREN.
OH!
AW!
AND I'M AFRAID THAT'S THE END OF MY STORY... FOR NOW.
I CAN'T BELIEVE PIRLIPAT TURNED ON HIM SO QUICKLY WHEN HE CHANGED INTO A NUTCRACKER!
IT'S AWFUL!
IF THE NUTCRACKER IS SMART, HE'LL SETTLE HIS SCORE WITH THE MOUSE KING AS SOON AS HE CAN.
BUT PERSONALLY, I HOPE WE CATCH THE MOUSE KING FIRST WITH THE TRAP GODFATHER IS MAKING US!

MARIE SLEPT SOUNDLY, DREAMING OF THE MOUSETRAP, UNTIL...
...THE MOUSE KING ARRIVED BY HER BEDSIDE AGAIN.
Chapter Ten
THE CURSE
AH, YOU EVIL LITTLE THING, YOU CAN'T GET RID OF ME SO QUICKLY! I'M NOT FOOLED BY TRAPS—I GLADLY ATE ALL THE FAT.
YOU'VE CROSSED THE LINE NOW, AND YOU'VE FAILED TO TRICK ME, SO TONIGHT MY WISHES MUST BE GRANTED TIMES THREE!
YOUR PICTURE BOOKS ARE WHAT I DESIRE—
LEAVE THEM FOR ME OR NUTCRACKER WILL END UP IN THE FIRE!
OH, I CAN'T KEEP ON LIKE THIS!
SOON I'LL HAVE NOTHING LEFT TO GIVE THE MOUSE KING!

THERE'S ALMOST NOTHING I CHERISH MORE THAN MY BEAUTIFUL BOOKS WITH ALL THEIR STORIES OF ADVENTURE AND FANTASY...
GASP!
NUTCRACKER!
WHAT HAPPENED?!
IS THIS MOUSE KING'S BLOOD? YOU DON'T LOOK HURT...
OH, NUTCRACKER, I KNOW YOUR WHOLE STORY NOW!
I KNOW YOU CAN HEAR ME, EVEN THOUGH YOU WON'T MOVE.
SO PLEASE KNOW THIS...
...I AM YOUR FRIEND.
YOU MAY DEPEND ON ME WHENEVER YOU NEED HELP.
AND I AM ALWAYS HERE FOR YOU. SO I MUST WARN YOU...
...THE MOUSE KING HAS BEEN THREATENING YOUR LIFE NIGHTLY!
HE DEMANDS MY FAVORITE THINGS IN EXCHANGE FOR YOUR SAFETY!
SOON I'LL HAVE NOTHING LEFT TO GIVE HIM!
WHAT WILL HE WANT NEXT?! MY MOTHER AND FATHER? WHAT AM I SUPPOSED TO DO?

MY LADY, MARIE STAHLBAUM!
OH, WHAT DO YOU OWE ME?
I AM JUST A WOODEN NUTCRACKER. I DON'T DESERVE THE KINDNESS YOU'VE SHOWN ME!
YOUR SACRIFICES FILL ME WITH SORROW. I AM FOREVER IN YOUR DEBT!
AND YOU ARE RIGHT, THIS IS THE MOUSE KING'S BLOOD!
HE WAS JUST HERE A MOMENT AGO! HE WILL LIKELY RETURN AGAIN SOON.
I SEE NOW THAT I MUST FINALLY FACE MY FEARS AND PUT AN END TO THIS CONFLICT! FOR YOUR AND YOUR FAMILY'S SAKE!
ALL I NEED NOW IS A SWORD.
WOULD YOU HELP ME ONE LAST TIME, MISS STAHLBAUM? WOULD YOU HELP ME FIND A SWORD TO DEFEAT THE MOUSE KING?
YES, OF COURSE!
OH, WHAT?
BACK TO A TOY?
I'LL GET YOU A SWORD, NUTCRACKER!
I KNOW JUST WHERE TO FIND ONE!
WAKE UP, FRITZ!
I NEED A SWORD!

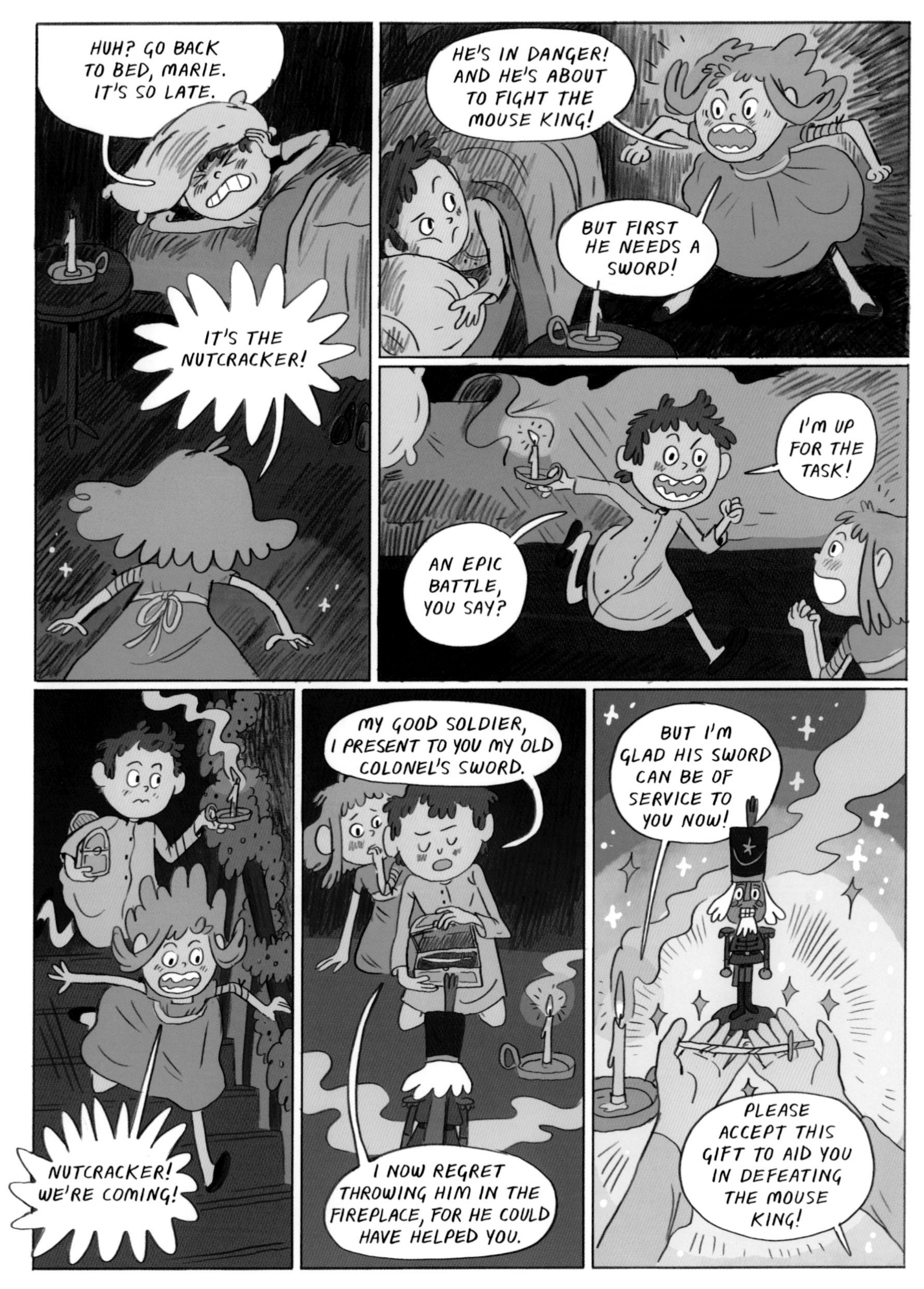
HUH? GO BACK TO BED, MARIE. IT'S SO LATE.
IT'S THE NUTCRACKER!
HE'S IN DANGER! AND HE'S ABOUT TO FIGHT THE MOUSE KING!
BUT FIRST HE NEEDS A SWORD!
I'M UP FOR THE TASK!
AN EPIC BATTLE, YOU SAY?
NUTCRACKER! WE'RE COMING!
MY GOOD SOLDIER, I PRESENT TO YOU MY OLD COLONEL'S SWORD.
I NOW REGRET THROWING HIM IN THE FIREPLACE, FOR HE COULD HAVE HELPED YOU.
BUT I'M GLAD HIS SWORD CAN BE OF SERVICE TO YOU NOW!
PLEASE ACCEPT THIS GIFT TO AID YOU IN DEFEATING THE MOUSE KING!

LET'S GO BACK TO BED, MARIE. ALL WE CAN DO NOW IS WAIT.
BUT MARIE COULD NOT FALL BACK TO SLEEP THAT NIGHT.
INSTEAD, SHE WAITED FOR THE CLOCK TO STRIKE MIDNIGHT.
SUDDENLY SHE HEARD STRANGE NOISES...
CLANG
CLANG CLANG
...LIKE DISTANT METAL HITTING METAL!
CLANG!
IT ALL ENDS HERE, NUTCRACKER.
MOUSE KING! I'M SO SORRY I STEPPED ON YOUR MOTHER, MOUSERINKS!
CLANG!
IT'S TOO LATE FOR SORRY, NUTCRACKER!
IT WAS AN ACCIDENT!
THAT DOESN'T MATTER ANYMORE! YOU AND THAT GIRL WILL REGRET CROSSING ME!
CLANG!
NO!
AGH!
YOU'LL BOTH BE SORRY WHEN I'M DONE WITH YOU!
GASP!

LEAVE MISS STAHLBAUM OUT OF OUR AFFAIRS!
WHOOOOOOSH!
AHK!!!
I'LL BITE HER CHEEKS AND SHE'LL BECOME A USELESS NUTCRACKER...
JUST LIKE YOU!
ARGH!
SHE CAN'T PROTECT YOU FOREVER!
I'LL NEVER LET THAT HAPPEN!
CLANG!
I'D LIKE TO SEE YOU STOP ME!
RAAHHHHHHHHH!!!
AAAAAAARRGGG!
eeee!
eeeee!
GASP!
OH! WHAT HAVE I DONE?
HISS!
EK!
HISS!
HISS!
EE!
AH!

I KNOW YOU CARRY THE BURDEN OF MOUSERINKS'S HATE.
BUT THIS WAS NEVER OUR BATTLE TO FIGHT!
CLANG
CLANG
CLANG
WE ARE BUT PAWNS IN AN OLD WAR.
I'M SO SORRY TO BE THE ONE TO DEAL YOU THIS AWFUL BLOW!
I KNOW I'LL NEVER FORGIVE MYSELF FOR MY ROLE IN YOUR FATE.
BUT I HOPE YOU CAN FORGIVE ME.
OH, NUTCRACKER!
YOU DID IT!
THE MOUSE KING CAN'T HURT US ANYMORE!
MISS STAHLBAUM!
DID YOU WITNESS THAT AWFUL SCENE?!

YOU FOUGHT SO BRAVELY ON MY BEHALF. THANK YOU.
YOU ARE MY DEAR FRIEND, MARIE STAHLBAUM. IT WAS YOUR MEMORY THAT FILLED ME WITH COURAGE AND GAVE THIS WEAK ARM STRENGTH.
YOU'VE SAVED MY LIFE YET AGAIN. I OWE YOU AN ENORMOUS DEBT.
AH, WELL, FRITZ HELPED A BIT, TOO...
...BUT, I AGREE, IT WAS MOSTLY ME.
I HAVE ONE LAST FAVOR TO ASK—WILL YOU TAKE THE SEVEN CROWNS?
IT'S DANGEROUS TO LEAVE THEM OUT FOR THE MOUSE KINGDOM TO FIND.
I KNOW YOU'LL KEEP THEM SAFE.
NOW THAT MY ENEMY IS VANQUISHED... I CAN FINALLY SHOW YOU MY KINGDOM!
YOUR KINGDOM?
YES! WHEN PRINCESS PIRLIPAT BANISHED ME, A NEIGHBORING KINGDOM HEARD OUR PLIGHT AND TOOK US IN.
MY FATHER BECAME THE KING-ASTRONOMER OF THE LAND...
AND, THEREFORE, I BECAME A PRINCE!
I LIVED THERE IN HAPPINESS WITH MY FRIENDS AND FAMILY...
...UNTIL THE MOUSE KING BEGAN HUNTING ME AND I HAD TO GO INTO HIDING. THAT'S HOW I ENDED UP HERE, PRETENDING TO BE A TOY!
I MISS MY HOME SO MUCH.
HOW FAR AWAY IS IT?
NOT FAR AT ALL!
OH, REALLY?
FOLLOW ME!

Chapter Eleven
THE PRINCE'S KINGDOM
HERE WE ARE!
THE COAT CLOSET?
IT'S A SHORTCUT!
THESE STAIRS LEAD TO MY KINGDOM.
WHO KNEW MY FATHER'S COATS HELD SUCH SECRETS?!
THERE ARE SO MANY THINGS I'D LIKE TO SHOW YOU, MARIE! THERE'S

IT'S SO BRIGHT!
LOOK, MARIE. THERE IT IS! MY HOME.
IT SEEMS SO FAR AWAY. DO YOU THINK WE CAN MAKE IT BACK HOME IN TIME FOR BREAKFAST?
MOTHER WILL BE SO WORRIED IF I MISS BREAKFAST.
TIME WORKS DIFFERENTLY HERE. WE'LL BE BACK WELL BEFORE THEN!
OH, HOW WONDERFUL. IT SMELLS LIKE FRESH ORANGES!
THE TREES IN ORANGE BROOK FOREST OWE THEIR SWEET SMELL TO THE FAIRIES WHO TEND THEM.

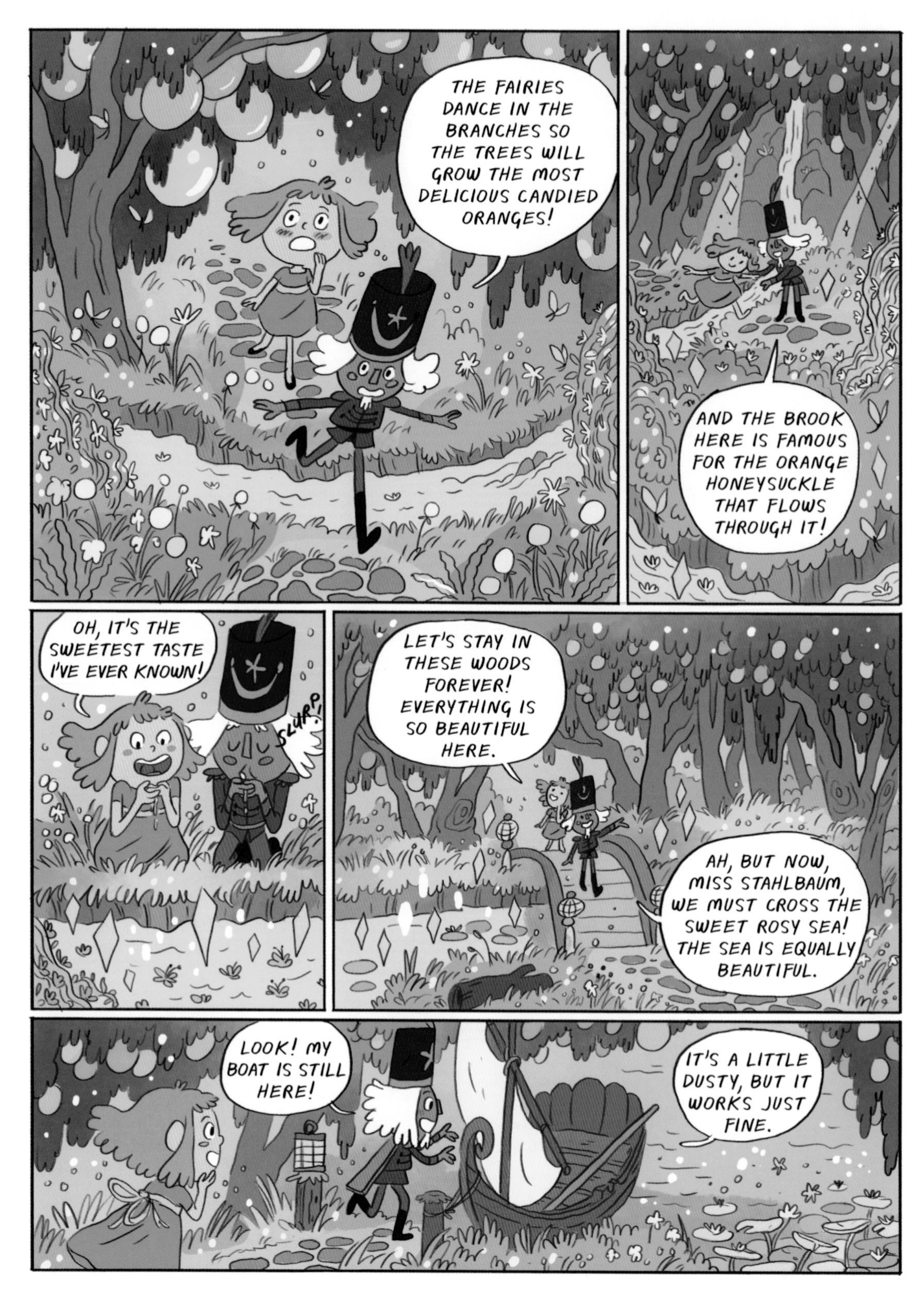
THE FAIRIES DANCE IN THE BRANCHES SO THE TREES WILL GROW THE MOST DELICIOUS CANDIED ORANGES!
AND THE BROOK HERE IS FAMOUS FOR THE ORANGE HONEYSUCKLE THAT FLOWS THROUGH IT!
OH, IT'S THE SWEETEST TASTE I'VE EVER KNOWN!
SLURP!
LET'S STAY IN THESE WOODS FOREVER! EVERYTHING IS SO BEAUTIFUL HERE.
AH, BUT NOW, MISS STAHLBAUM, WE MUST CROSS THE SWEET ROSY SEA! THE SEA IS EQUALLY BEAUTIFUL.
LOOK! MY BOAT IS STILL HERE!
IT'S A LITTLE DUSTY, BUT IT WORKS JUST FINE.

I'VE NEVER BEEN ON A SAILBOAT BEFORE!
WELL, WELCOME ABOARD, FIRST MATE STAHLBAUM!
MY FATHER TAUGHT ME TO READ THE STARS, AND MY MOTHER TAUGHT ME TO SAIL! I SHOULD FIND MY WAY HOME IN NO TIME.
BUT I'LL NEED A FIRST MATE TO HELP ME NAVIGATE!
I'LL HELP YOU!
I LOVE SAILING! EVEN THOUGH I'VE ONLY EVER SAILED IN MY DREAMS...
THIS LITTLE FISH IS GIVING ME A ROSE!
YES, THAT'S HOW WE KNOW THEY'RE DIRECTING THE WINDS IN OUR FAVOR!
WHY, THANK YOU FOR THIS GIFT, MASTER FISH!
THEY'RE SINGING A BEAUTIFUL SONG FOR US.
SAILING ON THE ROSY SEA MEANS MUSIC WITH EVERY CREST OF A WAVE.
WHO SAILS WITH US ACROSS THE ROSY SEA?
THE NUTCRACKER PRINCE AND THE FAIRY SILVER-TREE!
O'ER THE WAVES THEY ARE GOING, GOING
WHILE THE SWEET SUMMER WINDS ARE FLOWING, FLOWING
AH! CAPTAIN, I SEE SOMETHING!
UP AHEAD! I THINK IT'S THE CASTLE!

YES! THERE IT IS—THE CAPITAL.
WOW!
WE'LL TAKE THE SECRET PASSAGEWAY IN. I DON'T WANT TO CAUSE A FUSS IN TOWN.
OH, THIS REMINDS ME OF THE GARDEN IN THE CHRISTMAS GIFT GODFATHER DROSSELMEIER MADE FOR US!
IT'S PROBABLY BECAUSE HE WAS INSPIRED BY MY HOME. HE'S VISITED MORE THAN ONCE, YOU KNOW!
HE HAS?
IT'S TRUE— HE COMES BACK HERE FROM TIME TO TIME.
HOW COME HE'S NEVER TALKED ABOUT IT?
I WONDER IF IT'S BECAUSE NO ONE WOULD BELIEVE HIM IF HE TOLD THEM.

HERE WE ARE. I CAN'T WAIT FOR YOU TO MEET MY PARENTS AND ALL MY FRIENDS!
THE PALACE IS JUST THROUGH THIS SECRET DOOR!
I'M SO EXCITED TO TELL THEM OF MY ADVENTURES AND YOUR BRAVERY!
pat pat
SIGH...
...HOME.
TWIST
FINALLY.
CCRRREEAAAK

Chapter Twelve
THE PALACE
HELLO?
I'M HOME!
IS ANYONE HOME?
HELLO?

HELLOOOOOOOOOOOOOO
ANYONE?
HELLO?!
I'M HOME!
HMM, I GUESS I'D HOPED FOR A WARMER RECEPTION...

I SUPPOSE WE DID COME IN THE SECRET WAY...
...BUT I WONDER WHERE EVERYONE COULD BE? USUALLY THE PALACE IS FULL OF PEOPLE.
I HEARD IT FROM OVER HERE!
OH, COULD IT BE?!
IS IT HIM?!
OH!
I HEARD HIS VOICE!
I SEE HIM!
THERE HE IS! OUR SON!
MOTHER! FATHER!
OH, DARLING!

OH, WE'VE MISSED YOU SO MUCH!
WE'RE SO GLAD YOU'RE HOME!
MOTHER, FATHER, I WANT YOU TO MEET SOMEONE!
THIS IS MY DEAR FRIEND MARIE STAHLBAUM!
HELLO, YOUR MAJESTIES.
SHE SAVED MY LIFE!
ON MORE THAN ONE OCCASION!
THE KING AND QUEEN WERE THRILLED TO MEET MARIE AFTER HEARING ABOUT THE STAHLBAUMS FROM THEIR BROTHER DROSSELMEIER.
AND THEY THANKED HER PROFUSELY FOR SAVING THEIR SON FROM DANGER AND LOOKING AFTER HIM WHILE THEY COULDN'T.
COME, I HAVE SO MUCH TO TELL YOU ALL!
MARIE, WILL YOU HELP ME TELL THE TALE OF OUR ADVENTURES?!
I'D LOVE TO!
AND SO THE NUTCRACKER AND MARIE TOLD THE COURT ABOUT THEIR TRIALS WITH THE MOUSE KING.
THE NUTCRACKER TOLD OF THE GREAT FIRST BATTLE BETWEEN THE TOYS AND THE MOUSE ARMY!
AND MARIE SHARED HOW SHE THREW HER SHOE TO PROTECT THE NUTCRACKER!
THEN SHE EXPLAINED HOW THE MOUSE KING VISITED AND DEMANDED SACRIFICES TO KEEP THE NUTCRACKER SAFE!

THE NUTCRACKER'S PARENTS QUAKED HEARING HIS TALE.
MARIE REVELED IN THE TELLING OF HER ADVENTURES ALONGSIDE THE NUTCRACKER.
A GREAT CROWD BEGAN TO GATHER TO HEAR MARIE AND THE NUTCRACKER'S TALE! THEY POURED IN FROM EVERY ROOM, CURIOUS ABOUT THE COMMOTION.
SOON, SEVERAL SERVERS WALKED AROUND WITH TRAYS OF DELICIOUS-LOOKING DELICACIES!
MARIE TRIED EVERY SINGLE DISH!

AND FINALLY, WITH MARIE'S HELP, I VANQUISHED THE MOUSE KING FOR GOOD!
SHE'S THE SAFEKEEPER OF HIS SEVEN CROWNS, SO HE'LL NEVER BE ABLE TO TORMENT OUR PEOPLE EVER AGAIN.
JUST AS MARIE BIT INTO THE MOST DELICIOUS FRUIT SHE'D EVER TASTED...THE ROOM BEGAN TO FILL WITH FLUFFY CLOUDS.
WHAT'S HAPPENING?!
NUTCRACKER! WHERE ARE YOU?
MARIE SUDDENLY FELT VERY ALONE.

Chapter Thirteen
THE DREAMER
MARIE...
...MARIE, IT'S VERY LATE!
HOW CAN YOU SLEEP SO LONG?
BREAKFAST HAS BEEN READY FOR HOURS! IT'S COLD BY NOW.
OH! THE DELICACIES FROM THE NUTCRACKER'S KINGDOM MUST HAVE MADE ME FALL ASLEEP!
* YAWN *
THE NUTCRACKER'S KINGDOM? MARIE...

YOU WON'T BELIEVE ALL THE BEAUTIFUL THINGS I SAW! THE PALACE WAS—AND THERE WERE ORANGE FAIRIES—AND NUTCRACKER IS A PRINCE AND—
IT SOUNDS LIKE YOU HAD A BEAUTIFUL DREAM, MARIE.
BUT NOW IT'S TIME TO FORGET ALL OF THAT AND START YOUR DAY.
BUT IT WASN'T A DREAM.
MARIE, MY PATIENCE IS GROWING THIN OVER ALL THIS NUTCRACKER NONSENSE.
BUT IT'S NOT NONSENSE! IT'S ALL TRUE! DROSSELMEIER'S STORIES ARE REAL! YOU **MUST** BELIEVE ME!
MARIE, STOP THIS AT ONCE!
NOW, WHAT'S THIS?
DROSSELMEIER'S STORIES HAVE COMPLETELY INFECTED MARIE'S BRAIN.
I'M CALLING HIM OUT OF HIS WORKSHOP.
MARIE, DID YOU HAVE A NIGHTMARE?
NO! I VISITED THE NUTCRACKER'S KINGDOM AND MET THE KING AND QUEEN AND SAW INCREDIBLE THINGS!
I'M NOT MAKING ANY OF IT UP!

LOOK! I EVEN HAVE PROOF!
WHAT PROOF COULD YOU POSSIBLY HAVE, MARIE?
YOUR MOTHER'S RIGHT—THIS NEEDS TO STOP.
LOOK! THE MOUSE KING'S SEVEN CROWNS!
HMM?
WHEN THE NUTCRACKER VANQUISHED THE MOUSE KING, HE ENTRUSTED THE CROWNS TO ME!
THAT WAS RIGHT BEFORE HE SHOWED ME THE SHORTCUT TO HIS KINGDOM THROUGH THE COAT CLOSET!
OH?
MARIE, DARLING, TELL ME WHERE YOU GOT THESE, REALLY.
I DON'T WANT ANY MORE LIES.
BUT WHAT SHOULD I SAY, THEN? I'VE ALREADY TOLD YOU!
IT WOULD BE A LIE IF I TOLD YOU ANYTHING ELSE!

WHAT'S THIS? AM I IN TROUBLE AGAIN?
KNOCK KNOCK
MARIE HAS MADE UP A WILD STORY ABOUT HOW SHE CAME TO HAVE THESE TINY CROWNS.
HMM? LET ME SEE...
DID YOU GIVE THEM TO HER? THEY LOOK LIKE YOUR HANDIWORK.
AH! WHAT AN EVIL PACK! WE DROVE THEM ALL BACK! FOREVER GONE, THE WAR IS WON! PURRUM PURRUM PURRUM...
GASP!
GODFATHER DROSSELMEIER! PLEASE TELL THEM ABOUT THE NUTCRACKER AND HIS BEAUTIFUL KINGDOM! PLEASE TELL THEM IT'S ALL REAL!
TELL THEM WHERE I REALLY GOT THE CROWNS. THEY'LL ONLY LISTEN TO YOU!
SADLY, DEAR MARIE, I CANNOT.

LISTEN TO ME, MARIE. YOU MUST DRIVE THIS FOOLISHNESS OUT OF YOUR HEAD, ONCE AND FOR ALL.
YOU SCARED YOUR MOTHER AND ME TO DEATH WHEN YOU BROKE THE GLASS IN THE CABINET.
THEN YOU WOKE UP FRITZ TO MAKE HIM GIVE YOU A SWORD. AND NOW ALL MY NICE COATS ARE ON THE FLOOR DOWNSTAIRS.
THIS HAS TO STOP.
I FORBID YOU TO EVER SPEAK OF THIS DREAM AGAIN.
AND IF YOU DO... I'LL HAVE NO CHOICE BUT TO THROW THE NUTCRACKER OUT THE WINDOW.
NO!
...BUT...
YES, FATHER.
AND SO MARIE RESIGNED HERSELF TO SITTING BY THE WINDOW ALL DAY, DREAMING ABOUT FANTASTICAL LANDS, THE WAY SHE HAD BEFORE DISCOVERING THEY WERE REAL.
SHE THOUGHT ABOUT ALL THE BEAUTIFUL THINGS SHE'D SEEN...
...AND HOW THEY WOULD NOT BE FORGOTTEN SO EASILY.

DAYS PASSED, AND STILL SHE COULDN'T KEEP VIVID DREAMS OF THE NUTCRACKER'S CANDY KINGDOM FROM HER MIND.
SINCE SHE WAS NO LONGER PERMITTED TO SPEAK OF HER ADVENTURES, SHE BEGAN DRAWING THEM IN THE MARGINS OF HER PICTURE BOOKS SO SHE WOULDN'T FORGET THEM.
THE NUTCRACKER WAS KEPT LOCKED AWAY IN THE CASE DOWNSTAIRS. ALL MARIE COULD DO WAS LOOK AT HIM THROUGH THE GLASS.
ONE MORNING, WHILE DROSSELMEIER WAS BUSY REPAIRING A CLOCK IN THE FRONT ROOM, MARIE SAT LOST IN HER DREAMS, LOOKING AT THE NUTCRACKER BEHIND THE GLASS.

DEAR NUTCRACKER, IF YOU TRULY ARE ALIVE, I WANT YOU TO KNOW...
...THAT I WOULD NEVER HAVE BEHAVED AS PRINCESS PIRLIPAT DID WHEN SHE SAW YOU TRANSFORM INTO A NUTCRACKER.
I HOPE THAT YOU KNOW...I WOULD NEVER SLIGHT YOU LIKE SHE DID.
YOU NEVER, NOT ONCE, CEASED BEING AN HONORABLE AND WORTHY PRINCE TO ME.
FIXED!
KNOCK KNOCK KNOCK
hm?
AH, THAT MUST BE THE VISITOR I'VE BEEN EXPECTING!
A VISITOR?

MY NEPHEW! HE'S JUST ARRIVED FROM VERY, VERY FAR AWAY!
DROSSELMEIER, YOU NEVER TOLD ME YOU HAD A NEPHEW.
HAVE YOU FORGOTTEN?
THE NUTCRACKER! HE'S VANISHED FROM THE CABINET!
MARIE, THERE'S SOMEONE HERE I'D LIKE YOU TO MEET!

Chapter Fourteen
THE NUTCRACKER

NUTCRACKER?
IS IT REALLY YOU?
MISS MARIE STAHLBAUM, I HAVE TRAVELED MANY LONG MILES TO BE HERE TODAY.
NUTCRACKER!!
I CAME TO THANK YOU FOR BELIEVING IN ME.

IT WAS IN THIS VERY ROOM THAT YOU SAVED MY LIFE, AND FOR THAT I AM FOREVER GRATEFUL TO YOU.
AND JUST NOW, YOU SAID MOST AMIABLY THAT YOU WOULD NOT HAVE TREATED ME AS PIRLIPAT! YOU BELIEVED IN ME, AGAINST ALL ODDS...AND IN THAT MOMENT, YOU BROKE THE SPELL!
SO I'VE ALSO COME TO ASK IF YOU'D LIKE TO BECOME A PRINCESS IN THE ROYAL COURT!
ME? A PRINCESS? REALLY?
IT WOULD BE SO WONDERFUL TO HAVE YOU IN THE PALACE! WE COULD GO ON ADVENTURES THROUGH THE CANDY KINGDOM ALL THE TIME!
PLUS THERE ARE MANY OTHER PRINCES AND PRINCESSES AT COURT WHO WOULD LOVE TO BE YOUR FRIENDS!
WOW!

EVERYTHING'S TURNED OUT JUST AS THE PROPHECY SAID. IT'S ALL BECAUSE OF YOU, MARIE!
AND YOU DID IT ALL ON YOUR OWN. THANK YOU FOR BREAKING MY NEPHEW'S SPELL.
I KNEW IT! I KNEW IT WASN'T JUST A DREAM!
A DREAM?! OF COURSE NOT!
WOW, THANK YOU, NUTCRACKER! I WOULD LOVE TO COME WITH YOU. BUT WHAT ABOUT MY PARENTS...AND FRITZ? MAY THEY COME, TOO?
YOUR PARENTS AND FRITZ ARE INVITED, TOO! YOU'LL ALL BE WELCOMED INTO THE ROYAL COURT!
WE CAN GO NOW, AND EVERYONE WILL MEET US THERE!
IN THAT CASE, LET'S GO!
GODFATHER DROSSELMEIER, WILL YOU COME, TOO?
I'LL BE RIGHT BEHIND YOU!
THIS WAY. MY CARRIAGE AWAITS US, YOUR MAJESTY!
OH, HOW LOVELY!

FROM DREAMS DO DREAMERS FLOCK.
TICK TOCK, TICK TOCK, TICK TOCK...
A TRUER HEART WAS FOUND IN NONE...
MOUSE KING'S LOST, AND WHIMSY'S WON.
THOUGH MOUSERINKS'S SPELL WAS DEEP AND CRUEL...
...WARMTH AND LOVE HAVE COME TO RULE.

AT LAST PEACE AND HARMONY PREVAIL...
...SO IMAGINATION MAY SET SAIL.
AND SO NO LONGER MUST I ROAM...
...I TURN MY HEART BACK TOWARD MY HOME.
WITH BLUEST SKIES OF WONDER SEEN...

...ONLY BY THOSE WHO FOLLOW DREAMS.

ONCE UPON A TIME...
...THERE WAS A BEAUTIFUL PRINCESS...
...WHO LOVED TO LET HER IMAGINATION WANDER...
AND SHE DID SO TO HER HEART'S DELIGHT.
THE END

Author's Note

The tale of Marie and the Nutcracker has been a beloved Christmastime story for children and adults for generations, and over the last two centuries it has been adapted by countless artists. First it was a popular German novel by E.T.A. Hoffmann, then years later it was repopularized in English by Alexandre Dumas, whose version of the story was adapted by Marius Petipa, Lev Ivanov, and Pyotr Tchaikovsky into a wildly successful ballet. It has been adapted for the screen numerous times—once, in fact, while I was in the midst of drawing this book. As I worked on the art, the story's history and popularity proved an unshakable weight, despite support from my ever-encouraging editor and peers. I often wondered how I could possibly be qualified to retell this story, especially alone, while whole teams were remaking *The Nutcracker* with incredible visuals in different mediums.

Nevertheless, I was irresistibly drawn to this story. After reading Marie's tale, I had to share my vision of it. I was simultaneously frustrated by the wandering plot and romantic themes of E.T.A. Hoffman's original story and obsessed with its perfection as a fever dream. I loved it and hated it and wanted it changed and wanted it kept intact. I was completely sucked into this dark, bizarre story with a girl's imagination at its core, and found I wanted to focus my retelling on that. Marie's bending reality was fascinating to me, and I was disturbed by the ways she was shamed for it. And I connected deeply with Marie in the moments when she was forced to hide her dream world within herself for fear of losing the only fantasy and comfort to which she could retreat.

That's the Nutcracker story I wanted to tell.

Like Marie, I grew up with an imagination I was told to suppress. While I read Hoffmann's *The Nutcracker and the Mouse King*, I was reminded of the adults who treated my drawings and stories like a sickness that needed to be medicated. If I drew on my class notes, I was scolded for not paying attention; if I doodled on my homework, I was sent home with a note to my parents; and even in art class, if I sketched what I wanted, my teachers would insist I draw realistically or not at all. Marie's story reminded me of the characters I let flourish only in my own time, away from others, fiercely protecting the right to keep and grow them for myself without consequence. Of how they became my deepest and oldest friends, who guided me when I was lost or needed consoling. I recognized Marie's struggle, and I wanted to be a part of telling it in any way I could.

Ultimately, I realized that this story could be retold a thousand times and it would still have meaning for each new reader. My hope is that, in giving life once again to Marie's grand imagination, I can encourage readers who see themselves in Marie to cherish and pursue their own dream worlds. I hope readers of her story, especially those who feel the same unshakeable connection that I did, will always feel empowered to take risks and be creative, even if their dreams seem daunting.

—Natalie

Published by First Second
First Second is an imprint of Roaring Brook Press,
a division of Holtzbrinck Publishing Holdings Limited Partnership
120 Broadway, New York, NY 10271

Don't miss your next favorite book from First Second!
For the latest updates go to firstsecondnewsletter.com and sign up for our enewsletter.

Library of Congress Control Number: 2018953660
ISBN: 978-1-59643-681-7

Our books may be purchased in bulk for promotional, educational, or business use.
Please contact your local bookseller or the Macmillan Corporate and Premium Sales Department
at (800) 221-7945 ext. 5442 or by email at MacmillanSpecialMarkets@macmillan.com.

First edition, 2020
Edited by Calista Brill and Rachel Stark
Cover design by Andrew Arnold
Interior book design by Molly Johanson
Printed in China by Toppan Leefung Printing Ltd., Dongguan City, Guangdong Province

Digitally penciled, inked, and colored in Photoshop on a Wacom Cintiq.

Based on *The Nutcracker and the Mouse King* by E.T.A. Hoffmann

1 3 5 7 9 10 8 6 4 2